AUG 0 0 2023

KEY
PLAYER

KEY PLAYER

A **FRONT DESK** NOVEL

KELLY YANG

SCHOLASTIC PRESS / NEW YORK

Library of Congress Cataloging-in-Publication Data available
ISBN 978-1-338-77625-6

1 2022

Printed in the U.S.A.   23
First edition, September 2022
Book design by Maeve Norton

TO EVERYONE WHO HAS EVER
STRUGGLED IN P.E., LIKE ME

CHAPTER 1

I read in a book once that if you want something bad enough, all you have to do is picture it. Then BOOM, it becomes reality.

I have always been a very good picture-er. After all, I pictured my family and friends buying a motel and running it together. I pictured that business would thrive. Before all that became a reality, when my parents and I first moved from China to California, I pictured that I would master English as a second language.

So it shouldn't be so hard to picture myself scoring a goal in PE—or at least getting anywhere near the soccer ball. Even now that my family has health insurance and I'm not so afraid of getting hurt, I still can't help avoiding the ball like it's radioactive.

Maybe it was all those years of sitting on the sidelines, or the fact that my classmates all had twice the sports equipment I had. (Do you know how expensive shin pads are?!) But when Mr. Antwell said, "All right, kids! We're going to be doing a soccer unit in honor of the World Cup, which as you know is coming up, and being played right here in LA!" I instinctively looked around for a cooler of ice to bury my head in.

The only cup I was interested in was a cup of jasmine tea, along with some time to write my next piece for the school newspaper.

But instead, on this scorching hot day, Mr. Antwell marched up to me on the field and yelled, "Mia, what are you doing? This is soccer! You're walking around the field like it's a museum!"

"I'm sorry," I muttered. "I was thinking about a column I'm going to write!"

"Well, think with your feet!" Mr. Antwell cried. "C'mon, picture yourself as Brandi Chastain, dribbling the ball and driving it into the goal!"

I shook my head. How did I tell Mr. Antwell I *couldn't* picture myself as Brandi Chastain? First of all, she looked nothing like me! She had wispy hair the color of glistening sand, while mine was thick and jet-black. Second, even if I *did* dribble the ball, I'd probably end up kicking it off the metal corner of the goal, have it come flying back at me, and get sent to the emergency room with a concussion. I still remembered the time my mom had to go to the hospital. It was expensive *and* she had to take days off work. Even with health insurance, none of us could afford time off for a PE head injury.

"I need water," I told Mr. Antwell.

Bethany Brett, my forever nemesis, rolled her eyes and groaned, "We'll never win with Mia on our team!"

"It's not all about winning," I fired back, huffing and puffing to the side of the field toward our water bottles. My friend Jason glanced over at me and raised a concerned eyebrow, silently asking, *You okay?* He'd gotten so fast, I could barely see his feet when he ran. PE was much more his thing. I nodded back: *I'm fine.*

As I sat down to take a long drink, I pictured myself in San Francisco over winter break, at the new journalism camp that the *San Francisco Tribune* was hosting. It would be so amazing. I'd actually get to write, *all day*! But the camp was expensive, and

I needed a scholarship. And for that I needed straight As. *Including* in PE.

With a sigh, I put my water down and picked myself back up. As I walked over to join my classmates, all huddled together, kicking their feet, their bold legs darting in and out as they chased after the ball, I marveled at their bravery. None of them ever seemed to even think about getting hurt. They just *played*. I wished I could do that. But no matter how good my imagination was, I couldn't erase all the years of worrying every time the ball came close to me.

I looked at the grass, fighting the urge to plop back down and read instead. It probably didn't help my speed that I had a book tucked inside my PE shorts.

Mr. Antwell blew sharply on his whistle. "Mia! You done with your water break? Let's hustle! I want you to play like it's *you* at the Rose Bowl in two weeks, in front of millions of fans!"

Yeah, right. Me playing in the Rose Bowl? Selling hot dogs, *maybe*.

Still, I tried to pick up the pace, for Mr. Antwell's sake.

"She can't run—look at her toothpick legs!" Bethany complained.

"Hey!" Jason cried out in my defense.

My cheeks grew hot, and I looked down. My legs were skinny, sure, but why'd Bethany have to say *toothpick*? I kept jogging, and of course, that's exactly when my copy of the Baby-Sitters Club #2 decided to fall out of my waistband.

Mr. Antwell blew his whistle again, stopping the game. He walked over and stared at my book on the field. All my teammates crowded around. I knew I was DOOMED.

"Mia Tang. You brought a *book* to soccer?" Mr. Antwell asked.

Bullets of sweat rolled down my forehead. Journalism camp flashed through my mind. San Francisco! The Golden Gate Bridge! All my hopes and dreams! I glanced in the direction of the locker room, but Lupe was late again. She was usually late coming back from the high school, where she went for math, and frequently missed PE. Today, I missed her more than ever. Even with Jason here, I felt so alone.

"I . . . uh . . ." I had to say something! "I was using it as a weight! To run faster," I finally managed. "You know, like in those commercials on TV!"

"Uh-huh." Bethany rolled her eyes.

I ignored Bethany and looked up at Mr. Antwell. "I swear, I wasn't gonna read it. I already know what happens in the book!"

That part was true. The Baby-Sitters Club was one of my favorite series. They couldn't release the books fast enough, and I would reread them over and over again while I waited for a new one to come out.

Bethany crossed her arms. "Aren't those books about, like, super-annoying girls who kidnap little kids?"

My jaw dropped. "*No!* It's about girls who start a babysitting club to make money!"

I knew Bethany was just being mean, as usual—but I couldn't help it, I felt extremely protective of the characters. Especially Claudia Kishi, who was the only Asian American girl I'd ever seen on the cover of a novel.

Mr. Antwell just shook his head at me with supreme disappointment. As I reached for my book, Mr. Antwell blew his whistle again. "Leave it!" he ordered.

"But it's a library book!"

"I said *leave it*!"

So I jogged away, staring back longingly at the book on the grass. At the piece of myself that just didn't fit, no matter how hard I tried on the field.

. . .

I couldn't get my book back until lunch break. At least by then, Lupe had returned from the high school and could walk with me.

"So, I guess I missed something?" she said.

I looked down, kicking the grass with my Payless sneakers. There was a hole the size of a quarter in the sole of the right shoe, but we were saving up to buy a house, so I didn't want to tell my parents.

"Mr. Antwell still screaming at you?" she guessed.

I nodded. "How about you? Those girls treating you any better?"

Lupe's face fell. I knew this semester wasn't easy for her either. She didn't have to deal with Mr. Antwell's wrath most days, but she did have *high school girls*, who liked to ask Lupe questions about boys that she didn't understand, then laugh when her face turned red.

I didn't know how Lupe did it. I could barely handle the brats our own age like Bethany! But Lupe was determined to keep pursuing her math dreams.

"They're still the same," she said. Then her eyes flashed. "But guess what? My teacher recommended me for the Math Cup!"

I stopped walking and grabbed her arm. This sounded like a cup I could get on board with! I pictured a huge yogurt parfait with numbers. "YESSSSS!!!" I screamed.

Lupe giggled. "Have you heard of it? It's this major competition, and everyone on the team is a junior or a senior," she said, jumping on the grass as we reached the field. "Including Ethan Thompson."

"Who's Ethan Thompson?" I asked.

"This guy with dimples who all the other girls like," Lupe explained.

I smiled. "Do *you* like him?"

"No. But maybe they'll finally be nicer to me now that I'm on the same team as him." Lupe waggled her eyebrows.

I chuckled. Sounded like a plan.

"Just hope I don't flame out . . ." Lupe said, her face clouding with worry again.

"Are you kidding? You're going to *rock this*! When do you guys start?"

"Next week!" Lupe said.

"Who's the coach?" I asked. "Maybe my mom knows her!"

Now that Mom was teaching full-time at the high school—she had her own classroom and everything!—she went to all the faculty meetings.

"Him. Mr. Jammer. I haven't met him yet, but I hope he likes me."

"He will," I assured her. We got to the patch of grass by the goal and looked around. Thankfully, my book was still lying in the same place I'd been forced to leave it. Tenderly, I picked it up and dusted off the grass.

"How mad did Mr. Antwell get at you for this?" Lupe asked.

"Mad." I made a face. "You don't think he's gonna give me a bad grade, do you? Because that would jeopardize *everything*."

"Relax. It was just one class," Lupe said.

I chewed my cheek. "How long do you think the soccer unit's gonna last?"

"At least till the World Cup's over. Oh, hey, that reminds me! I heard they're putting World Cup blankets on all the beds of the hotels in Pasadena! You think we should do that?"

"Nah," I said. "What would we do with them after?"

The last thing I needed was a bunch of blankets reminding me that I was totally uncoordinated, even in my sleep.

Just then, I looked up and saw Mr. Antwell crossing over from the track to talk to us. I quickly put the book behind my back.

"Hey, Mr. Antwell," we said.

"Mia, can I have a word with you?"

I handed my book to Lupe, then walked over to Mr. Antwell, trying hard not to study the number of frown lines around his mouth when he looked at me.

"What's up?" I asked.

"Mia, I really need you to take PE seriously," he said, crossing his arms.

"I do take PE seriously," I insisted. "I'm just not that good at sports."

"Because you don't want to be—"

"No," I interrupted. "I *do*. It's just . . ." My voice trailed off. How could I explain that my arms were as rusty as an old bike chain because for years, my parents told me every day not to get anywhere close to the ball because we didn't have insurance? I couldn't. It'd be way too embarrassing.

"I'm a good writer, though. . . ."

"You can't just be good at one thing, Mia." Mr. Antwell put on a pair of sunglasses, even though he already had one on top of his head. I didn't know which one to look at. I felt like they were doubly reminding me of the fact that I was bad at sports.

"Why not?" I furrowed my eyebrows.

"Because it's not healthy!"

I wanted to ask *why not?* again. But I knew Mr. Antwell was a one *why not?* per day kind of guy.

He sighed. "I just want you to know, when you get your report card this week, that I still believe in you."

My heart started punching my chest.

"What grade did you give me?" I asked.

"Well, you'll see," he said.

"Please? I don't want to wait." I shook my head frantically. Report cards weren't due for *three days*. Three whole days wondering and panicking! PE might finally send me to the emergency room—not for running, but for stress!

Mr. Antwell shifted his weight from one foot to the other uncomfortably. I could tell he really didn't want to tell me. But he'd opened Pandora's box, and there was no putting the GRADE issue back inside.

Gently, he took off his sunglasses again. And as he told me my fate, I felt the field underneath my feet open up and swallow me whole.

CHAPTER 2

I stumbled backward and fell on the dry grass. The sharp, stiff blades poked my palms. Sitting there and staring up at Mr. Antwell's shadow towering over me against the blinding sun, I saw my dreams dissolve like the clouds.

There goes journalism camp. There goes my dream of going to San Francisco and meeting Amy Tan, the only author I know who looks like me, and spreading my wings as a writer.

"I'm getting a *C*?" I whispered, pushing the tears back.

"C means average. A C is generous."

Ouch. "Mr. Antwell, you don't know how much I need this grade," I begged, scrambling to my feet. "I'll do extra credit!"

I started running in place, pushing my knees high just like Mr. Antwell always instructed us. I was so desperate, my knees nearly punched me in the face.

"Mia, stop. How about you just get closer to the ball? Maybe even touch it once in a while?" Mr. Antwell asked. "It's not going to hurt you."

I dropped my arms—and knees—and sighed.

"I expect a better effort from you next term," he said sternly, then turned to walk away.

To his back I cried, "But I want to make a better effort *now*!"

It was too late. Mr. Antwell didn't turn around, and as the lunch bell rang, I dragged my toothpick legs off the field. Lupe tried to cheer me up with a handful of Jolly Ranchers on the way back to class, but the sadness still pooled in my chest.

I wished my legs worked as well as my fingers.

I wished my arms were as strong as my mind.

Most of all, I wished Mr. Antwell saw me for the things I was *really* good at, and not for the things I couldn't control.

• • •

That afternoon behind the front desk at the Calivista Motel, I put my backpack down and glanced at the stack of fan mail waiting for me. Now that I was a regular columnist for a student newspaper in China and a staff writer for the school paper I'd started with my friend Da-Shawn, I received a lot of fan mail. Usually, the sight of letters from my readers made me bounce happily on my stool for hours. Today, I pushed them to the side. Reading them now would just make me sadder about not being able to go to the *Tribune* camp.

Dad walked in from the manager's quarters. He added a bunch of keys to the wall, each representing a freshly cleaned room.

"Hey! How was school?" Dad asked, reaching for a reusable shopping bag lying by the desk.

I shrugged.

Excitedly, he pulled a light green rain jacket out of the bag. "You like it? I got it at a yard sale today. Three dollars!" He put it on and grinned. Dad loved bragging about the good deals he got from yard sales.

"You went to a yard sale in the middle of the day?" I asked. "Without me?"

"I was out looking for houses," he said. Now that Mom had her stable high school job and the motel was doing well, my parents were determined to purchase our first American house. The manager's quarters that the three of us shared as an apartment was getting cramped.

Mom wanted a kitchen island. She had watched all these American TV shows to improve her English, and in every single one, they had a kitchen island. Mom wanted one not just for cooking, but to sit at while she graded quizzes. And she and Dad both wanted to be able to sleep through the night without having customers come knocking. Even with our sign saying that we were closed after 11:00 p.m., night-owl customers still came by. It got so bad that Mom had to move into one of the guest rooms.

"Did you find anything?" I asked him.

Dad shook his head and sighed. "Nothing with a fireplace." He was as fixated on getting a fireplace as Mom was on a kitchen island— and as much I was fixated on getting a dog.

Everyone else in my class had a dog. Kristy in the Baby-Sitters Club had a dog. Even my cousin Shen in China now had a dog! I wanted my own, to keep me company when I wrote. But Mom and Dad said I couldn't have one at the Calivista, in case a customer was allergic.

Dad took off his new green jacket and held it up against me to see if it would fit. I wriggled away.

"What's the matter? It's going to be chilly up in San Francisco!"

I bit my lip and didn't say anything.

"It'll keep you nice and warm when you're exploring Angel Island," he continued. "That's where they kept some of the earliest

Chinese immigrants. You should see their messages etched into the wall—"

I wished Dad would stop talking about all the things I was dying to do and now couldn't. I put my hand over my stomach and quickly excused myself. "Sorry, Dad, I'll be right back."

I rushed through the manager's quarters, squeezing by the boxes of hoisin sauce and dark soy that Jason ordered for the Calivista restaurant, East Meets West, to make his signature dishes.

Then I bumped into Jason himself as I walked out the back door.

"Mia! Wanna try our new kimchi cashew rice?" he asked. "Hank and I made it!"

"Maybe later," I replied, turning away—but not fast enough.

"Are you okay?" Jason asked.

"Uh-huh!" I said brightly. I took my hand off my stomach and pretended all was well. I didn't want to get into my grades with Jason. I just wanted to pretend the C wasn't happening for a little while longer.

As I kept walking to the staircase, he called out, "Can we talk later?"

"About what?" I asked.

"About the restaurant . . . I've just been thinking a lot." I turned and saw Jason bite his lip. "About my future."

"Sure," I told him. "Later!"

Finally, I got to the bottom of the back staircase. It was the one place I could let my feelings out, where I could let myself be weak. Everywhere else, I had to be strong.

I had to be strong for Dad, who didn't think we'd ever have stable jobs, and now we were about to buy our first American house. I had to be strong for Mom, who didn't think she could become a real teacher or that I could become a real writer. I had to be strong for everyone's dreams.

But here at the back staircase, I could be weak for me.

As the tears pooled in my eyes, I told myself the same thing I told myself every time I sat here: *It's going to be okay.* And: *There's always next year's camp.*

Hank spotted me and walked over from his old room. Over the summer, he'd purchased a nice new condo, right near the lake. It was his pride and joy, and he got to see the Disneyland fireworks every single night from his living room. But he still kept a room at the motel for nights when work at East Meets West ran late.

"Mia?" he asked.

I didn't bother to wipe my tears away. Hank and I go way back; he's allowed to see me weak too.

"Hey," I said.

"What's wrong?" he asked, taking a seat next to me. He was holding a piece of paper.

I sucked in a breath and started telling him about my grade. The shame choked in my throat.

Hank patted my hand. "I feel like every time we're sitting on this staircase, it's because of a grade. And every time, you know what happened?"

"But this time's different. This time, there's nothing I can do about it." I pointed at my legs. "I can't kick any harder or run any faster, not even if you put one of those heat lamps under my feet!"

Hank laughed. "No one's getting powered by heat lamps here," he assured me. "But you can try talking to your teacher. Tell him how much this grade means to you."

"I already did. No use."

Hank put a hand to his chin. "Well, maybe it's time to go over his head," he suggested.

I looked at him. "You mean go to my counselor?"

Mr. Ingleton was always eating nuts at assembly—*loudly*—even though we were a nut-free school. I'd never been to his office for anything.

"It's worth a shot," Hank said.

Hank was right. I'm Mia Tang. I may be the slowest person on the soccer field, but I'm the first person to defend my dreams. And I wasn't about to give up just like that! I jumped to my feet.

"Great idea!" As I leaned over to give Hank a hug, I glanced down at the piece of paper in Hank's hand. It was his secret recipe for his signature saltine burgers.

Hank *never* wrote out his secret recipe.

"What's that for?" I asked.

Hank grinned. "This here is *my* journalism camp," he declared. Beaming, he told me that a very fancy restaurant, the Pasadena Grill, had called. They had heard about his burgers and wanted to see if he wanted to partner with them. "Just imagine! They have the scale, the distribution, the money to take my food nationwide—Mia, this is the moment I've been dreaming about! It's time to take the Hank show to prime time!"

I giggled as we both thrust our fists into the sky.

"To prime time!!!" we both shouted.

CHAPTER 3

My knees jiggled as I sat across from Mr. Ingleton in his small, windowless guidance counselor's office. I'd brought a stack of my columns for him, thinking he might be interested in reading them. On the phone last night, Da-Shawn had said, "Show 'em what you got, Mia!" But when I told Mr. Ingleton why it was so important I pull up my grade in PE, he hardly glanced at my writing, reaching instead for another handful of nuts.

"So let me get this straight," he said. "You're here because you got one bad grade in PE?"

"It's not just a bad grade. It means I can't go to this journalism camp. All my grades have to be—"

He silenced me with his almond-dusted hand. "I get it. They wanna make sure you're well-rounded."

I'd heard that term before, but I never really knew what it meant. I glanced down at my tummy in the chair, rising and falling with nerves. It looked perfectly round to me.

"As in, not just a bookworm," he clarified.

Hey! I frowned at him, offended. I was proud of my reading. I even had a T-shirt that said *Professional Bookworm* on it that I got at a yard sale!

"Programs like that want to groom future leaders. And in order to be a leader, you have to be good at everything, not just one little thing."

"I wouldn't call writing 'one little thing,'" I muttered.

He gave me a look, and I fell quiet. I reminded myself of the immense power that counselors had. They could see everyone's grades. They could even break the nut rule!

"Look, it's nice that you like writing," Mr. Ingleton went on. "But that can't be all that you're about. Sports is about character building," he said. "It's about teamwork. Every great leader this country's ever had has been good at sports. That's what it takes to be all-American."

I furrowed my eyebrows, more confused than ever. Was he saying I wasn't American? I reminded him that my parents and I just became citizens. "I even have my new passport—I can bring it to you. Would you like to see it?"

"No thanks. That's great, but I'm not talking about a piece of paper. I'm talking about the mentality, the tradition. High schools and colleges in America, they're interested in more than just a homework robot."

My cheeks burned. "I'm not a homework robot," I whispered to the floor.

"Sorry, a *writing* robot. Same thing," Mr. Ingleton said, reaching for another handful of nuts.

. . .

That afternoon, I edited student submissions for the school newspaper and tried to toss Mr. Ingleton's words out of my head. Da-Shawn was out interviewing the school janitors for a story over lunch, so I was in the News Room all by myself.

The News Room used to be our district bus drivers' lounge, but then they got their own waiting room and facility in the district office. So Da-Shawn and I lobbied hard for the room—much to Bethany and her friends' annoyance. They'd wanted to convert it into a recording studio. Thankfully, the school agreed with me and Da-Shawn, even putting in a computer and a printer for us to produce the school newspaper.

I added commas and periods to articles, but stuck in my mind, like the sticky coat of dry roasted peanuts that you can't get off your hands, were the counselor's phrases.

Homework robot.

Bookworm.

And the one that stung the most: *all-American.*

If I wasn't good at sports, did that mean I wasn't completely American? Then what did that make me? All-nothing?

Da-Shawn walked in just then and put his camera down on the table.

"You wouldn't believe what the janitors told me," he said excitedly. "They've had to remove a hundred and fifty wads of gum from under the—" He took a look at me. "What's wrong?"

I put my editing pen down. "Forget gum wads. You know what we should do a story on? Whether PE should be optional. I mean, why do we have to prove ourselves by running the mile and playing soccer if that's not what we're good at?"

Da-Shawn looked shocked. "PE is, like, my favorite class!"

Da-Shawn was one of those well-rounded people Mr. Ingleton was talking about—an amazing writer *and* an incredible athlete. He could run the mile in less than seven minutes. *And* conduct an interview while he sprinted.

"Well, it's not mine," I muttered.

For me, PE was minutes of standing around, worrying whether anyone would actually pick me for their team, feeling like day-old bread in the bakery.

"But you get to be part of a team!" Da-Shawn protested.

"So? I'm part of a team now," I said, pointing at him and me. "This here. This is a team."

Da-Shawn nodded, though I could tell he wasn't convinced. A news team wasn't the same as a sports team. There was just something magnetic about sports. Feverish, almost. And it was only going to get worse as the World Cup got closer.

. . .

Mom was at the kitchen table in the manager's quarters when I got back to the Calivista.

"How was school?" she asked.

I reached for a bag of prawn chips on the counter. Then put it back and picked up a can of Pringles instead. Would *that* be more American? I hated that I was even wondering.

"Don't eat too many of those. I'm making *mapo tofu* for dinner, your favorite," Mom said, looking up from her papers.

I smiled. She usually had so many staff meetings after school, Dad and I just ate at the motel restaurant.

"That's great. How come you're home so early?"

"I needed a break. The staff meeting was exhausting," she said, putting her pen down and closing her eyes. I walked over and started to massage her tired, full-time-teacher shoulders.

Slowly, Mom told me about the guy in her faculty meeting who wouldn't let anyone else talk.

"I didn't even have a chance to present my new activities," she said, disappointed. I knew she was extremely proud of the games she'd invented to make math equations easier to remember for her kids.

"I'm sorry," I said.

"I'm beginning to think it's not about who works the hardest, but who talks the loudest," Mom sighed. "And my English . . ." She let her voice trail off.

Apparently I wasn't the only one confused about the rules for success.

"Your English is *fine*," I told her.

Mom reached up a hand and patted mine with it. I could tell she appreciated the words but didn't entirely believe me.

"Anyway," she said. "Some mapo tofu will take my mind off things. You want to help me make it?"

I nodded eagerly. As Mom got up to wash the tofu, I ran out back to the restaurant.

"Hey, Jason, you got an apron I can borrow?" I asked.

"Sure!" he said.

As he looked around, I asked, "So what did you want to talk to me about?"

"Oh, nothing, it can wait."

Jason? Wait? Now I was *really* curious.

He finally found an apron and handed it to me. Then, taking a breath, he said, "It's just—I've been thinking, and, well, I love the Calivista restaurant so much. Especially working with Hank. I'm always telling my dad how much I love working with him. But . . ."

Oh, no. He's not quitting, is he? My heart jumped to my eyelashes.

"But?" I prompted.

"Well, it's just that I feel like I've contributed a lot to it," he said.

"You totally have!" I agreed. People lined up around the block all summer for his food. Even Mr. Yao, Jason's grumpy dad and our old boss, was impressed. He's been coming around, watching Jason cook.

"I guess what I'm saying is, you, Hank, Lupe—I mean, you guys all own a piece of the Calivista. I wish I could be part of it too. Officially."

Wow. I was *not* expecting that.

"How long have you been thinking about this?" I asked him.

"Only every day. For the entire summer."

"Oh."

"I just want to be a part of the thing I helped build, you know?"

"Of course," I started to say. It made total sense. Jason had worked so hard, along with Hank, to put East Meets West on the map. He was directly responsible for the booming business and the thrilled investors. And we had *so* many investors. What was one more?

"I don't see why you couldn't be an investor," I said. "But where would the money come from?"

I knew Jason made a killing in tips, but the value of the Calivista had gone up so much; to become an investor required serious cash now.

"Don't worry about it." Jason waved the question away.

Uh-oh. I narrowed my eyes.

"Okay," he said finally. "I'd get it from my dad."

Oh, no. After what we'd been through with Mr. Yao—we'd worked so hard to get out from under his thumb! We couldn't possibly let him back in! I shook my head.

Jason added quickly, "It doesn't matter either way—it's *my* money!"

"No it's not; it's your dad's!"

"So?"

"So it means *he'll* be an investor. That's not happening."

I twisted the apron in my hands as I turned to walk back to the manager's quarters, panicking at the thought of Mr. Yao owning part of the motel again. Jason scurried after me.

"You're not even going to think about it?"

I turned around. "I have. I thought about it when your dad worked my parents to their bones. And docked their pay whenever something broke. When he refused to let them leave the motel together, not even to go to parent-teacher conferences with me! When he kicked Hank out. You want me to keep going?"

"It would just be his *money*, not him!" Jason insisted.

"Money talks," I snapped.

I walked into the manager's quarters and slammed the door behind me as Jason called out, "That's exactly what my dad said you'd say! But I told him you were a fair leader, a good leader!"

I leaned against the back of the door, squeezing my eyes shut. I could feel my resistance waning as Mr. Ingleton's words came back to me yet again—to be successful in America, you had to be a good leader. Was I a bad one for wanting to protect my family?

"Hey, you get the apron?" Mom called from the kitchen.

"Yep," I said, walking back inside.

"What's wrong?" Mom asked.

Washing my hands, I told Mom what Jason was asking for.

"Letting Mr. Yao back in . . . I don't know. . . ." she said, shaking her head and making a long sound through her teeth.

"I know! What about Hank and all the rest of us? Are we supposed to just forget?"

Mom reached for the scallions. I tried to help her cut some, but the kitchen was tiny and we kept bumping into each other.

"Can't say I blame Jason," Mom said. "He wants to be part of something."

"He *is* part of something."

"You know what I mean," Mom said. I bumped into her accidentally again, and some of the newly sliced scallions fell out of her hand. "We really need a bigger kitchen," she sighed. Across the room, *Full House* was on TV. Mom stared enviously at their kitchen island.

"Then we can make smoothies together," I said with a smile.

Mom chuckled. "Be like real Americans!"

My smile faded. I wanted a kitchen island as badly as she did. But I thought we already *were* real Americans. If only the goalposts didn't keep moving.

CHAPTER 4

Later, I found Hank out by his car, putting his recipes and ingredients together into a briefcase.

"Hey! How'd it go with your counselor?" he asked me.

I made a face.

Hank held open the passenger side door. "Let's go for a ride."

I hopped in, and the delicious aroma of Hank's saltine burgers and tomato fries wafted from the back seat. The fries were something he'd invented that summer as a healthy substitute for french fries. And man, were they good! Hank made them out of green tomatoes dipped in buttermilk and cornmeal, with just a touch of cayenne pepper for an extra kick.

I reached for one and nibbled on it. The light crunch temporarily distracted me from my troubles. But then the juices settled and reality came crawling back.

If Mr. Yao owned the Calivista again, would we still be able to just jump in the car and take off somewhere?

"What's the matter? Too salty?" Hank asked.

I shook my head. "No, your fries are always perfect." Hank turned onto the 5 Freeway, and soon we were passing the Disneyland exit. I thought about going there for the first time that summer with Lupe and Jason. It had been the best day of my life. We were the Three

Keys! And now one of the keys was sad because he didn't feel like an equal.

I told Hank everything as he drove.

"Wow." Hank whistled. "Mr. Yao back in the picture—who would have thunk it?"

"Why can't Jason just be happy with the way things are?" I asked. "He gets paid and he gets all these tips—"

Hank gave me a look.

"Mia, you and I both know being an employee and being an owner—that ain't the same thing. The boy wants to feel like he's working toward something." Hank pointed to the back seat, at his recipes and sample burgers. "He wants to advance himself, just like me."

"But this is Mr. Yao we're talking about!"

I thought about all the times over the summer that Mr. Yao had stopped by, looking for Jason. Each time, I'd bristled like a hedgehog.

"It's a risk, for sure," Hank agreed. "But you gotta look deep inside and ask yourself, how much of this is your pride holding you back? Sometimes you gotta take a chance if an employee is really worth it. Even if it's hard. Even if it's scary."

"Wow, Hank."

"What?" He chuckled at the way I was marveling at him.

"I'm just amazed. After how he treated you . . ." During our first year at the Calivista, the way Mr. Yao spoke to my parents and Hank—it made me want to kick a thousand soccer balls straight at his head.

"Well, I've been working with Jason in the kitchen every day," Hank said. "And I can tell you. He ain't his dad."

As Hank turned off the freeway, I noticed a giant billboard. It had a life-size poster of soccer superstar Mia Hamm kicking a black-and-white ball. It read:

TEAM USA vs. TEAM CHINA: FIFA WOMEN'S WORLD CUP—PASADENA ROSE BOWL, OCT 26

I studied Mia Hamm's long ponytail and perfect smile, all larger than life. Team China wasn't even on the sign.

"Not a big soccer fan, eh?" Hank asked, following my gaze.

"It's just a game," I muttered. And even though my parents were excited that Team USA was playing against China, it wasn't like we were getting tickets. I couldn't wait until the match was over and we could go back to playing baseball in PE. At least then I could sit way out in left field with my book.

"But, Mia, it's a historic moment. China versus the US—you don't see that happening every day!" Hank said. "That's gotta make you proud. Besides, I bet it would be pretty cool to write about for the school paper." He bumped his fist against my arm. "How's that going?"

"Good!" I said, smiling. I told Hank about the interviews I'd been doing—including the major profile on our inspiring librarian entitled "Believe in Your Shelf!"

And then I started thinking. What if I wrote a piece on the World Cup? An article so great, it blew my PE teacher's socks off—would Mr. Antwell change my grade? Better yet, what if I scored an *interview*?

"Hey, you think I could talk to one of the players?"

Hank pointed up at yet another Mia Hamm billboard. "Those superstars? The security's gonna be tighter than the entrance line at Disneyland."

"What about Team China?" I asked.

"*Now* you're talking." He tapped the steering wheel. "I'd love to know what those women are feeling right now!"

I would too! Coming to the US, playing at the Rose Bowl, going up against Mia Hamm and Brandi Chastain. That had to be exciting! My mind was exploding with questions.

"Where do you think they're staying?" I asked Hank, scanning the streets. "Can we find them?"

"Must be in Pasadena somewhere," he said.

I pressed my face up against the window, pointing to the Hilton, then the Hyatt, then the Westin. "Could they be in there? What about in there?"

Hank laughed. "Guess we'll have to check all of them. Lucky for you, we're in the biz. And I'm going to be spending a lot of time in Pasadena!"

I smiled at Hank. "Does Jason know about your deal with the Grill?"

"Ain't no deal yet," he reminded me, glancing back at his burgers. "But if we do land one, it'll be his deal too!"

"That's generous of you."

"Of course! We're partners!"

I glanced over at my friend, who said it with all his conviction. Jason had become more than just a colleague to him. He'd become his friend, his family.

And that's when I knew what I had to do.

CHAPTER 5

Hank and I walked into the Pasadena Grill with all his recipes and burgers in take-out boxes. The Grill looked nothing like our own diner, which was super casual and relaxed. This restaurant had big, heavy mahogany leather chairs at each table, and overhead hung a giant chandelier that looked like tiny crystal raindrops were falling from the ceiling. In other words, it was one of those places that looked too expensive to even go to the bathroom.

The hostess stared at us. "Can I . . . help you?" she asked.

"Yes, I'm Hank Caleb," Hank said cheerfully. "I'm here to see Roger Wamble, the manager?"

I gazed out at the dining room. "Oh my God, is that Robin Williams?" I whispered.

"Are you here for the busboy position?" the hostess asked.

"Uhhh . . . no," Hank said, embarrassed.

The hostess picked up the phone and called the manager. Then a second later, she smiled at us. "Right this way."

We followed her down the hall until we got to an office.

Mr. Wamble, a tall, lanky white man with a bow tie, came out to greet us. His suit looked as old and pricey as the chairs in his restaurant.

"You must be Hank," he said as they shook hands. "Thanks for coming up. And is this your . . . daughter?"

"I'm his colleague," I said. "My name's Mia."

"A very small colleague!" he remarked.

I felt my cheeks heat up as I stuck out a hand. But Mr. Wamble barely touched my fingers before pointing at Hank's take-out boxes. "I can't wait to try your famous burger! Is that it?"

"Got it right here!" Hank said proudly, opening a box.

"And the recipe?" Mr. Wamble asked, taking a burger.

Hank slowly retrieved a stack of papers from his briefcase. He smiled, but I could tell he was uneasy.

Mr. Wamble took a big bite. "Wow, this is really spectacular," he said. "I can see why so many people like it! The crunch! The texture!"

I grinned. "You should try it when it's piping hot! It's even better!" I said.

"I can make it for you. Right now!" Hank said. "We got time!"

I nodded.

Mr. Wamble shook his head, put the burger down, and dabbed his mouth with a napkin. "That won't be necessary. Just leave the recipe with me. I'll have the kitchen guys make me another one tomorrow, steaming hot. I promise." He motioned with his hand. "Can I take a look at the recipe?"

Hank hesitated. "You think we should sign a contract or something first?"

Mr. Wamble put a hand on Hank's back. "Contracts are for lawyers. We're foodies."

"Sure, but—"

"If we're going to be working together," Mr. Wamble said, looking into Hank's eyes, "we have to trust each other."

"Of course. But don't you think—"

"Trust is *very* important. It's the base ingredient for everything," Mr. Wamble continued.

Hank nodded. "I know . . . but this recipe here, it's kinda my baby. I spent a lot of time perfecting it over the years. Some of the stuff in here, I put in when I barely had a stove in my room."

"Which is why I want to get it *just* right." Mr. Wamble held out his hand, clearly growing impatient.

Hank glanced at me. "I think I'd rather make it for you myself. I can come back tomorrow."

Mr. Wamble huffed. "You know how many people come in here asking if we'd consider putting their dish on the menu?"

"How many?" Hank asked.

"Half a dozen a day," Mr. Wamble informed him. "And of those, you know how many we actually ask to see the recipe?"

Hank stared at him blankly.

"One percent," he told him. "Our clients are sophisticated. Important. We have actors and senators coming in. They're not just looking for a bite. They take big meetings here. Just yesterday, we had the president of the FIFA World Cup association, talking about the big match."

My ears perked up at the mention of the World Cup. "Did any of the players come?" I blurted. "Do you know where they're staying?"

Ignoring me, Mr. Wamble went on to Hank. "You have a real opportunity here. A chance to step up your game. But in order to do this, we have to take the *first* step. This is about give-and-take. A little give, and a little take. That's how this works."

Hank looked down at his recipe. I could tell how conflicted he was—everything he'd ever taught me about doing business said *don't hand the paper over!* Not without a contract. Not without any terms. But in that moment, Hank was thinking about the goal. And how delicious it would be if he scored one with the Pasadena Grill.

Heart pounding, I watched as my friend handed over his most prized blueprint to Mr. Wamble.

CHAPTER 6

Driving back from Pasadena, Hank and I were both on fire, lit with the adrenaline of possibility.

"Can you imagine the mayor of Los Angeles sitting down and discussing race relations over one of my burgers?" Hank asked. "Wouldn't that be something?"

"Or the two women's soccer teams!" I beamed. "You think they'd ever share a meal? Or is that not allowed, you know, because they're enemies?"

"They're not enemies," Hank said. "They're athletes. Brave young women, trying to prove themselves in a sport. That's what's so great about events like the World Cup—they unite people."

I sure hoped Hank was right. America and China were my two worlds, so the two of them coming together at the Rose Bowl meant a lot to me. I was starting to think of the World Cup less as an impossible PE thorn under my foot and more as an opportunity.

"How much do you think tickets cost?" I asked Hank.

Hank whistled. "World Cup tickets? A couple of Benjamins, at least."

"You think they'd give a discount to a student reporter?" I pulled out my Student Press badge from my backpack. Da-Shawn and I had made them together and gotten them laminated at Office Depot.

"Maybe," Hank said. "But I'll tell you what, if this new partnership with the Grill takes off, I'll take you."

"Really??" I screamed with excitement.

Hank grinned, turning off the freeway and driving down Coast Boulevard toward his condo, where we'd grab a few more boxes of saltine crackers and other ingredients before heading back to the motel.

"What do you think Wamble's going to say when he finds out there are crackers in there?" Hank asked as he pulled into his parking spot. The saltines were what gave Hank's burgers their signature crunch. They were his secret ingredient!

"That you're a total genius!" I said to Hank, getting out of the car and following him to the door. As I walked, I added, "Still can't believe you gave him your recipe."

"I know," Hank said, his face clouding temporarily with worry. "But what's that thing Lupe used to say? You can't win if you don't play?"

I smiled as Hank opened the door. They were words that had carried us further than any of us ever expected. And now here we were, standing in the hallway of the brand-new, two-story condo Hank purchased with his Calivista money. Bright sunshine shone in through tall windows as Hank led me into his kitchen—a kitchen with a marble kitchen island, I might add.

I marveled at Hank's new digs. The kitchen was finally big enough for all of Hank's cooking. It had two ovens—so he could make a main course *and* dessert at the same time! I walked around the island, feeling the cool, smooth marble with my fingertips, wondering when my mom would have hers. I couldn't wait.

"What's it like, waking up in your own house every day?" I asked.

He thought for a long while, holding the saltine packages to his chest. "Like your heart's at peace," he finally said. "After years of it hammering like you got a hamster stuck in there."

I put my hand over my own chest hamster.

"I'd like mine to stop hammering too," I said. Then I sighed and admitted, "Especially when I think of Mr. Yao possibly coming back." The thing about living where we worked was, whenever there was a change, I worried twice as hard.

Hank picked up the rest of the ingredients. "Nothing's going to change, Mia. . . ."

Quietly, I admitted the other worry that had been stewing ever since Hank handed Mr. Wamble that burger.

"What if they give you, like, *big* money? You're not going to go running off to the Pasadena Grill, are you?"

There was no doubt Hank deserved it. That it should be him sitting inside that mahogany-wood office instead of Mr. Wamble. But I'd miss my friend so much.

"I'm not going anywhere," he said seriously. "You can bet your last saltine on it."

I smiled.

• • •

It was the middle of the dinner rush when we got back to the motel, and the first thing we saw was Mr. Yao, trying to convince his son to go home. But Jason insisted on holding down the fort.

"Oh, thank God, Hank, you're back," Jason said. "We've got eight more tables of people waiting."

"He can handle it by himself," Mr. Yao butted in. "C'mon, Jason, let's go home. The Lakers are on tonight!"

"I don't care about the Lakers," Jason said, taking the saltines from Hank and starting to crumble them. Hank grabbed an apron and put it on, then hustled to greet the customers.

"But that was *our* thing," Mr. Yao muttered, staring down at the coffee cup in his hands, but Jason was already out of earshot.

"Don't worry," I told Mr. Yao. "My dad can give him a ride home later."

Reluctantly, he put the mug back and reached for his keys. "I'm not *worried* about Jason," he said. "I just . . . miss him."

He looked so sad, I wanted to hand him a cracker. But every last one had been mushed up by Jason.

• • •

Later, after the last customer had left, Jason caught up to me behind the counter. I helped him stack all the new bottles of miso and sesame oil next to jars of saltine crumbs. He looked at me nervously as he worked.

"So . . . have you thought about what I asked?"

I nodded. "I just have to clear it with all the investors—" I started.

"But what do *you* think?" he asked. "Do I have a chance to be a part of this place or not?"

I put all the sesame oil down. It broke my heart that he even had to ask. Of course he should be a part of this place. This was *his* restaurant.

"Yes," I said.

Jason was so surprised, he jumped in the air, causing the sesame oils to tumble. I laughed.

"Really?" he asked.

I nodded eagerly, grabbing all the jars before they landed on the floor. "Just promise me your dad's not going to have a cow every time we take a break. Like when I go to Pasadena to find the Chinese women's soccer team!"

"I promise!" Jason cried.

"You ready to go home?" Dad asked, walking in. "And what's this about the Chinese women's soccer team?"

Excitedly, I told him my interview plan.

"That would be incredible!" he said. "They just landed! It was all over the Chinese news!"

"Did it say where they're staying?"

"Probably somewhere close to the Rose Bowl. And cheap," Dad said. "They don't have a lot of money, unlike the US Team. Women's soccer is still in its infancy in China. Some of the women worked in a factory before they joined the team."

My eyes boggled. "In a factory? Really?"

Dad nodded. "The goalie, Gao Hong, at least."

"And they made it to the World Cup?" Jason asked, as shocked as I was. "How'd they do that?"

"I'm going to find out!" I declared. This was my chance to prove to my PE teacher that I *did* care about sports. I cared a lot! My strengths just lay off the field—and that was okay!

Jason grinned as he tossed me an extra doughnut our dessert chefs, Carmela and Tanya, had made. It had a soccer ball on it. As I closed my eyes and bit down on the deliciousness, I felt a rush of sugar and possibility.

CHAPTER 7

That Saturday, Lupe and I sat at the front desk and pored over maps of Los Angeles. We were working with a thick directory of hotels that Hank got from the tourism office. When Lupe heard of my plan, she said she wanted to come with me.

"Aren't you going to be busy with the Math Cup?" I asked.

Lupe put the map down. "Let's just say, we don't exactly stand a chance."

"What are you talking about?"

"Well, at our first meeting, the coach didn't even show up," Lupe explained. "The other kids were all just messing around. They found the remote for the classroom TV and put on a movie. Somebody even brought popcorn."

"Whoa!" I exclaimed. "And there were no adults there at all?"

Lupe shook her head. "We did zero math. I'm doing more math here trying to figure out how many hotels are in Pasadena!" She pointed at the list we'd made. There were 78 hotels in the greater Pasadena area, 119 if you included motels.

That's when I noticed that next to the list in her notebook, Lupe had written *Ethan*, with hearts next to it. I smiled and asked her, "So how's Ethan?"

Lupe moved the map over her doodle hearts, embarrassed.

"He's fine," she said quickly.

"It's okay if you have a crush," I told her. "Remember last year, when I liked Da-Shawn?"

My best friend shook her head. "I just wrote that to see what it was like. The other girls in class, they're always doodling guys' names. But I don't *like* him."

Oh.

Quietly, she added, "I mean, he's smart and everything. And his armpits don't smell like onions. I know because I sit next to him in Math Cup. But . . . I just don't like him. Or any boy, for that matter." She took a deep, labored breath. Her voice lowered to almost a whisper. "Is that weird?"

I shook my head. "No. Of course not."

Lupe swallowed hard. I had no idea it was weighing on her this much.

"You should see the other girls in high school," she said, her voice practically a whisper now. "They're always putting on makeup and talking about boys. They look at me like I'm a weirdo."

I chewed my lip, feeling bad my best friend felt this way. I wanted to tug her back to the middle school. But at the same time, I knew how advanced Lupe's math skills were—she was really at the high school level, at least with numbers.

"You're not a weirdo," I said. "You're the most brilliant mathematician of all the mathematicians in the world!"

Lupe chuckled.

"And one day," I went on, "while you're riding your stretch limo to the Nobel Prize, the other girls will be like, 'Oh my God, I wish I knew that girl in high school. But I was too busy putting stained grease on my lips.'"

"And sand on my face!" she added.

I giggled, glad to be able to make her feel a little bit better. Then I told her what Bethany had said about my toothpick legs. Lupe wasn't the only one who worried about being a weirdo.

"And what if she's right?" I asked. "What if there's nothing I can do about it?"

I gazed down at my scrawny legs. Wishing they were faster. Wishing they were longer. Wishing they were hairier, even. The other girls were always talking about their changing bodies, while mine remained as basic as a featherless chicken.

"She's *wrong*," Lupe insisted. "Your legs are perfect."

I cozied up to my best friend, glad we could still have these soul-baring conversations. I hoped we could always talk like this. As we turned back to the maps, I asked, "So . . . is there someone you *do* like?"

Lupe shook her head. "That's the thing. I don't really like any-one," she said. "I keep waiting and waiting. You know the feeling where you get really close to a boy and you turn into a volcano inside?"

I nodded, still remembering it vividly from crushing hard on Da-Shawn last year.

"I don't get that," she said. "And I wish things could stay the way they are."

"Tell me about it," I replied. "Remember when PE used to be just running around, doing whatever we wanted?"

We both sighed, missing the good old days.

I flipped through the directory, stopping at the Grand Anza. It was the closest hotel to the Rose Bowl. I pointed it out to Lupe on the map.

"Should we go?" she asked.

Mom poked her head out from the kitchen. "You guys need a ride?" she asked. "I'm finally all caught up on grading!"

I thrust my arms up in the air. Mom was always so busy grading (whoever said teachers don't work on weekends?), it was rare to spend a whole Saturday with her. So I literally jumped at the chance to drive with Mom to Pasadena.

"Let's go!" I said.

Lupe reached for her backpack, and I grabbed my reporter's notebook, pen, and a Polaroid camera. If we managed to get the interview, Da-Shawn and my editor in Beijing would be so thrilled!

. . .

As she drove, Mom told us that when she was a girl, she'd wanted to play hockey. "I was lightning on ice! But the boys told me I couldn't," she said. "If these ladies win, it could change *everything* in women's sports in China."

"You think so?" I asked.

"Oh, I know so. Most people in China don't think girls should play sports. They believe a girl's role is not out on the field."

Lupe and I both rolled our eyes. "Where do they think it should be?" Lupe asked.

"In the house. At the piano. Trying to find a good husband."

We screwed up our faces.

"The point is, they're wrong," Mom said. "Look at these women and what they've achieved, all in the last twenty years, even with everyone around them telling them they can't do it!"

I rubbed my hands together. I couldn't wait to talk to them!

Mom asked Lupe how Math Cup was going.

Lupe sighed. "The coach, Mr. Jammer, didn't even show up."

"Mr. Jammer?" Mom turned to me in the rearview mirror. "That's the guy who's always talking in the meetings!"

"Well, he's not talking at the Math Cup meetings," Lupe said. "He hardly ever comes, according to the other kids. I guess he thinks, what's the point? We're going up against Sentilla Beach, and they have so much money. Plus *college* professors coaching them."

Mom got off the exit at Pasadena. "You mean to tell me you guys are up for the biggest math competition in the state, and you don't even have a coach?"

"We have . . . popcorn?"

Mom gave Lupe a funny look.

"One of the kids brought a big bag and . . ." Lupe groaned. "You don't want to know."

I could see my mom's problem-solving brain spinning hard. Finally, she slapped the steering wheel and declared, "That's it. First thing Monday, I'm going to go to the administration to ask if I can coach you guys!"

Lupe's eyes flashed. "YESSSS!!! That will be amazing!"

"I might not be the most experienced coach," Mom said. "But I got plenty of heart. And where there's a will, there's a way."

"Speaking of which!" I pointed at the majestic Grand Anza hotel sign up ahead.

Mom pulled into the parking lot, and Lupe and I shot out of the car.

CHAPTER 8

"Can I help you?" the receptionist at the Grand Anza's front desk asked. She was way more dressed up than I usually was at the Calivista desk, with a black suit and red silk shirt and her hair pulled back in a sleek bun. *Dang.* I was impressed.

"Hi," I said. "We're looking for some guests who might be staying here. Their names are Gao Hong, Liu Ailing, Sun Wen, and let's see . . . who else . . . ?" I had looked up the names of the soccer players in the local paper before we left. But before I could finish naming all the players, Sleek Bun stopped me.

"I'm sorry, *might* be? I can't let you know if someone is staying here." She frowned.

"Sure you can!" I said, pointing at her computer. I ran around and joined her behind the desk. I knew I could find it myself.

But Sleek Bun shrieked as if I was trying to rob her. "You can't be back here! This area is for staff only!"

"Jeez, okay, sorry," I said. "Habit."

I got back to the other side of the counter and whispered to Lupe, "What do we do?"

Lupe pointed and said, "Let's just sit in the lobby and wait."

I said thanks to the receptionist, and we walked over to the lobby lounge. Mom went to go check out the hotel spa. She'd never been to a spa before—that was another one of those all-American things she wanted to do, but it was much too expensive. Lupe and I found two big chairs and got comfortable.

My eyes were glued to the elevator doors.

"What are we looking for?" Lupe whispered.

"Chinese people," I whispered back. "Girls who look like they can take down Arnold Schwarzenegger. Anyone wearing Adidas."

"Got it," Lupe said, surveying the scene like a spy.

Unfortunately, the only people wearing Adidas were middle-aged vacationers. But a lot of them *were* talking about the World Cup match.

"I can't wait to see Briana Scurry crush those Chinese ping-pongs," an old man said. "They don't have a chance!"

"You don't think so?" his wife asked.

"Look at them, they were raised on rice and tofu!" he replied.

I stared down at my legs and arms—was *that* why they were so thin? My cheeks were heating up faster than Jason's oven.

Lupe jumped up. "What about rice and tofu?" she asked the man. "Are you judging people based on their character or their lunch?"

The old man swiftly pulled his wife away.

"I'll have you know rice and tofu are *delicious*!" I added.

"So's rice and black beans!" Lupe hollered. "With some pico de gallo!"

The security guard walked over to us. He cleared his throat, and we knew we were in trouble.

"The lobby's for hotel guests only. You guys have to leave."

"We were just sitting," I said. "Can't we sit?"

"No, this isn't a park," he replied. He pointed to a sign on the wall that said *No loitering*.

I furrowed my eyebrows. "We're not littering!"

Just then, Mom came out of the elevator. When she saw us getting booted by security, she informed him we were waiting for Gao Hong.

"Gao *what*?" the guard asked, screwing up his face.

"Hong!" Mom repeated.

I shook my head. I didn't know why Chinese names were always so hard for white people to pronounce. The security guard insisted there was no Gao Hong staying there. Mom asked if he was sure, which forced him to look it up.

Five minutes later, we were out of the hotel.

"Well, that's *one* way to find out," I said to Mom. Still, I was bummed. We'd driven all this way only to cross a single hotel off our list.

In the car, I told Mom what the old man had said about the Chinese players.

"I'm so sorry, honey," she said. "Sometimes people get carried away rooting for their favorite team."

But this felt like more than just rooting for their favorite team. It felt like he was putting down a part of *me*. Even though we didn't live in China anymore, I still ate rice and tofu.

I started to worry. If the match didn't unite my two sides, would it rip them apart? As Mom drove, I wrapped my arms around my body and hugged myself tight, clinging to all the pieces of me.

CHAPTER 9

It was nearly lunchtime when we got home. Lupe and I walked into the diner and climbed onto the counter stools. We gobbled up the dumplings Jason put in front of us, starved.

"Thanks so much again for letting me invest," Jason said. "Dad was STOKED when I told him the news. He's coming over right now with the check."

I reached for some water. The "coming over right now" part made my last dumpling go down a little funny. But it was official—Mr. Yao was back in. Late last night, I'd gotten all the investors to approve the deal.

"That's great," I said. "Is he going to be over here all the time?"

"Just Mondays through Wednesdays," Jason said. "We made a deal."

"He knows it's only for the restaurant, right?" Lupe asked.

Jason nodded enthusiastically. Since the Calivista motel and diner were technically one, we shared the same investors. It was important, though—to Lupe, my parents, and Hank—that Mr. Yao kept out of the motel business.

"Yeah, yeah, yeah, he knows!" Jason promised.

Mr. Yao's Navigator roared into the lot as if on cue. Lupe gulped down the last of her dumplings, and I picked up the bottle of vinegar, accidentally drinking *that* instead of water. Jason pushed open the diner door and skipped ahead to greet his dad.

We climbed off our stools and followed him outside.

"Hey, Dad!" Jason said. "Didja bring it?"

Mr. Yao grinned and pulled out a check from his wallet. He handed it to Jason, then surveyed the Calivista.

"Finally! We get to work as father and son," he said, throwing a glare to Hank. "As it always should have been. And spend some time together. How's my motel doing?"

"You mean your diner?" I asked, glancing at Jason.

"Diner, right, same thing!"

"It's doing great!" Jason beamed. I could tell how proud he was. Everything he'd ever done had led up to this moment. His dad finally accepted his dream of being a chef—not just accepted, but supported! With cold, hard cash! And we all knew how much Mr. Yao valued his cash.

Pushing the restaurant doors open, Mr. Yao frowned. "No, no, no, the setup here is all wrong."

"What do you mean?" Jason asked, gazing at the space he'd lovingly built. His eyes landed on the bright red counter stools he and Hank picked out after going to about five thousand yard sales. "You were just here last night!"

"As a customer. Now I'm an investor!" Mr. Yao said. "The stools are too spread out! You gotta squeeze them closer together so you can pack in more people. C'mon, let's try to make a little money here! And add some more tables!"

He continued walking through the restaurant, pointing and

suggesting. Mr. Yao had opinions on *everything*. How many paper towels we were using, where the trash cans were, even the brand of ketchup we used. By the end of the tour, Jason was clutching his hair with both hands.

I felt bad for my friend. But it was kind of funny to see Jason get a dose of what I had to go through all those years ago!

"Dad, it's not a big deal! We're doing fine here; everything's fine!" Jason yelped.

"Fine?" Mr. Yao scoffed. "I don't want to invest in *fine*. I want to invest in *big* and *bold*. Spectacular! And I know just how we're going to get there." Mr. Yao pointed at his son. "By hosting the Team USA victory dinner!"

Jason's and my jaws dropped at the same time.

• • •

During the break between lunch and dinner, Mr. Yao rearranged the tables in East Meets West, and I scrambled to find Jason. He was sitting by the back stairwell. He'd discovered my secret spot.

"How on earth are we going to get Team USA to hold their victory dinner here?" Jason asked. "And why does my dad always have to be so *critical*?"

I took a seat next to him and shook my head.

Jason scrubbed a soy sauce stain on his apron with a wet rag. "I actually thought he'd see how great I was doing. But he just keeps throwing targets that are completely over the top! Like what I've done already isn't good enough!"

Gently, I pried the apron from him.

"You don't have to listen to what he says, Jason. Just nod and say *uh-huh*, then forget it." I leaned over and lowered my voice to add, "That's what I did."

"But I want to make him proud!"

I guessed that was the difference between me and Jason. Mr. Yao wasn't my dad.

"You will," I said.

"Not now that he keeps setting impossible goals, like hosting the USA victory dinner!" Jason wailed. "They probably already have plans—at some Michelin-starred place in Hollywood!"

"First of all, we don't even know who's gonna win. . . ."

Jason turned to me. "C'mon, Mia, let's be real. America will beat China. We have to."

Once again, I felt the pieces of me jumping inside, clashing into each other. I didn't know how to get them to calm down.

"Why? Because China doesn't have fancy sponsors?" I asked.

"No, silly. Because Team USA's forward's name is Mia." Jason smiled.

I couldn't help but smile back. Even if I wasn't exactly—or even a little bit—like Mia Hamm.

I squeezed his apron, warm in my hands, as Jason nudged me lightly with his shoulder. "But seriously, don't you want your country to win?" His eyes searched mine.

I nodded eagerly. But then I thought of my mother's words, about how much it would mean to Chinese girls everywhere if Team China won. It could change the horizon of what we could and couldn't do.

"Wouldn't it be great if they both won?" I asked, handing Jason back his apron.

"That's impossible. It's the World Cup!"

I knew Jason was right. Still, walking back to the front desk and thinking about the article I wanted to write, I hoped that my readers would have room in their hearts for more than one story. I knew I did in mine.

CHAPTER 10

All night long, I kept getting the hiccups. The words *all-American* seemed to get bigger and bigger in my belly, leaving me with no room for anything else. I thought about what Jason had said too—*don't you want your country to win?*

Of course I did. America was my country now. Those women represented me as much as the Chinese women did.

In the middle of the night, I got up to look at that day's *Los Angeles Times*. I stared at the full-color picture of Mia Hamm. She looked so different from me. She had big, intense eyes and legs like a gazelle. Even her ponytail was different. It was thicker, with hair that flew like a sail behind her as she ran. We might have the same name, but she looked nothing like me. In fact, no one on the team looked just like me.

I turned the page. By comparison, the Chinese team had eleven people with hair and skin and eyes like mine. But they were from a place that my family wasn't a part of anymore. A place my parents left . . . for me. A place we couldn't always relate to, because we had changed.

We had become Americanized.

I crawled back into bed, wishing it was easier. Wishing my two identities weren't like two giant pillows underneath me, competing for one head.

* * *

Dad woke me up bright and early on Sunday.

"Get up! We've got five open houses today!" he said. His excitement was contagious, and I jumped out of bed, laughing. I could almost feel the wet nuzzle of my new puppy's nose.

Hank walked into the manager's quarters as my parents and I got ready.

"Remember, you gotta check the foundation," he told us as we wolfed down our tea eggs and congee. "See if there are any cracks in the sidewalk too. And no big trees within twenty feet of the house."

Hank was our real estate trailblazer, having already gone through this with his condo. He'd even taught us how to apply for a mortgage.

"Twenty feet. Got it," Dad said, opening the desk drawer and proudly taking out our preapproval loan paper. It was Dad's most treasured document, other than our citizenship papers. I hoped today was finally the day we got to use it.

"And you want a two-car garage, at the very least," Hank added.

"Let's hope our new place comes with that much land!" Dad turned to Mom. "Come on, let's go. Uncle Zhang and Auntie Ling are meeting us at the first place."

Uncle Zhang and Auntie Ling hadn't found a house yet either. Nor had any of my parents' immigrant friends. Every time someone wanted to make an offer, the house was snapped up by people with powerful, well-dressed agents. We didn't have a well-dressed agent, or any agent.

Mom grabbed her purse.

"Good luck. Early bird catches the worm!" Hank said, tossing me the Polaroid. "Take lots of pics!"

"We will!" I smiled at Hank, catching the camera and putting it in my backpack. In the car, I snapped pictures of myself making silly faces for my cousin Shen—he was on vacation with his parents in Sanya, a beach town in China, for fall break.

"Look! This one has a fireplace," Dad said, handing me the flyer.

"Who needs a fireplace? It's Anaheim," Mom said, fanning herself. Our car's air-conditioning was acting up again.

Our old Chevy creaked along on its last legs. It had served our family for years, having even been my bedroom at one point. But now its bumper was falling off and it made a strange *UGGHHEEEEK* noise whenever we drove too fast, like it was trying to cough. We desperately needed a new car. But my parents said, *One thing at a time*.

"A house with a fireplace—now that's the American dream!" Dad said. "We don't have to *use* the fireplace."

I gave him a funny look. We're judging nationality by house amenities now?

"I guess I can always use it to store my math worksheets," Mom said.

Math in the fireplace? Then again, this was the woman who used the dishwasher to store canned goods. I wouldn't put it past her.

Turning to me, Mom said she'd already made fifteen different exercises and five worksheets for the Math Cup team. "I looked it up, and the first competition is in a week!"

I bounced excitedly from the back seat. "In a week, really?"

"Careful, or the bumper's gonna come off again!"

I stopped bouncing immediately. We couldn't take that kind of chance, not with real estate agents checking out our car.

When we got to the first address, it was a small, pale one-story yellow house without a garage—just a single layer of wood, like a canopy, to park under. Mom and I got out while Dad parked on the street. We walked past the broken fence and crossed the yard, overgrown with weeds. The weeds filled my heart with hope—maybe this time, we actually had a chance!

As soon as we stepped inside the house, though, my excitement tanked. There was a *hole* in the living room roof! It was the size of a sofa. I walked over, stood under the hole, and took a picture of the blue sky.

"That's nothing," the agent said, walking over from the cellar stairs. "You could patch that up in no time. Or just leave it—enjoy looking at the stars at night!"

"What happens if it rains?" I whispered to Mom.

Mom told me to stand away from the hole, in case any pieces of the roof fell in. I took a few steps back, bumping into Dad. He was studying the fireplace.

"Does this thing work?" he asked the agent.

The agent held up his hands and said, "Everything is sold as is. No guarantees."

Dad poked at the fireplace, and a giant cloud of soot covered his finger. I spotted Uncle Zhang and Auntie Ling coming out of the kitchen.

"Is there a kitchen island?" Mom asked.

Auntie Ling shook her head. "Forget about an island. It doesn't even come with a stove!"

"No *stove*?" Mom asked.

I followed her into the kitchen. Instead of a stove, there was just a sign saying STOVE GOES HERE.

The agent insisted on showing us everything. "Close your eyes and just *imagine* the potential," he instructed as he led us into the master bedroom.

We weren't the only ones imagining. A family of ants was scurrying up the doorframe. Mom pointed at some of the black dots moving along the wall. "Are those ants?"

"I don't see any ants," the agent said, quickly squishing the ants with his thumb. "Those are just bread crumbs."

"Really? There's one on your head," Mom said.

The agent screamed, swatting at his face. I swallowed a giggle. When he finally brushed the ants off his cheek, he cleared his throat. "Anyway, for two hundred thousand dollars, all this can be yours."

"Two hundred thousand?" Mom wailed. "I thought it said a hundred and fifty thousand on the flyer."

"That's just the *asking* price," the agent said. "We expect to go well above asking."

"But there's a hole in the roof!" I protested.

"It's a seller's market," he replied.

The agent turned to my dad. "Talk some sense into your wife," he said. "This here's a good deal!"

Mom and I both shook our heads. No way were we living in this overpriced, hole-in-the-roof, stove-less anthill!

Dad informed the agent, "I don't need to talk any sense into her. She has plenty of sense, and her sense says *no thanks*."

. . .

Outside, Auntie Ling, Uncle Zhang, my parents, and I sat on the curb.

"I'm beginning to think we're never going to find a home," Mom mumbled.

Auntie Ling shook her head. "What is it with houses? They're either completely uninhabitable, or they get snapped up in crazy bidding wars."

"Let's face it, we can't compete," Uncle Zhang said with a sigh. "We can't even get a real estate agent. Last week, an agent kicked me out of his office after one look at my bank account."

Dad gasped. "But we already have the letter from the bank!" He pulled the loan letter out of his pocket.

"He said that's nothing. They give that out to almost everyone," Uncle Zhang said.

Dad's jaw dropped. He stared down at what a few minutes ago had been his most prized possession. Now it was reduced to the same worth as a used napkin.

"Agents want to see you have money in the bank. Cash. A lot of it, before they'll take you on," Uncle Zhang went on. "And after seeing my bank account . . ." He looked like he was about to cry. "He said he didn't want to waste his time."

I put my hand on Uncle Zhang's shoulder, feeling so bad for him. Dad kicked the pavement in frustration.

"That's ridiculous!" Dad exclaimed. "This paper *says* we can afford a house."

"Maybe we should just buy in San Gabriel Valley," Uncle Zhang suggested. "Where there are more Asians. I heard it's easier there."

I looked to Dad and shook my head. San Gabriel Valley was an hour away!

"Mia's school is here. So's the motel. We can't live all the way out there," Dad said, reaching for my hand. "We just gotta keep looking. We'll find something."

I turned around and took one last look at the crumbling house. I sure hoped Dad was right.

CHAPTER 11

When we got back, we found Mr. Yao at the desk, even though it was a Sunday and he wasn't supposed to come around until Monday. But that wasn't even the shocking part. The shocking part was he was actually answering phones. Now *there* was a sight I never thought I'd see.

Dad turned to me and said, "You better go take over. I'm gonna go find Hank. There *has* to be a real estate agent out there who wants to work with us."

Mom went back to her guest room to catch up on some work, and I ran inside the front office.

Mr. Yao hung up the phone as I walked in. "Where'd you guys go? You've been gone hours!" He gave me an annoyed frown.

"We were checking out houses," I said, showing him the flyer of the house with the fireplace. Even though we weren't going to buy it, I liked bragging about it to Mr. Yao. He didn't need to know about the hole in the roof.

"Houses are a lot of work," Mr. Yao harrumphed. "Like my garage. We were trying to do some renovation, and now there's a leak!"

"Oh, no!"

"Totally flooded. Smells like Jason's PE shorts cooked in vinegar."

I wrinkled my nose. "Is that why you came over here?"

"No. I came over here to see Jason," Mr. Yao said. "But he's too busy doing inventory to talk to me." He pointed at me and asked, "Why do you guys want to get a house, anyway? You live here!"

"We *work* here," I clarified. With a shrug, I added, "And we want a place of our own."

"Since when?"

"Since my parents can't sleep!" With a sigh, I told him about how there were always customers knocking on the window, even with the sign up.

"That's great! That's how we make money!" he protested.

"We can still make money—during business hours," I assured him. "We'll always be here first thing in the morning, just like Hank!"

"But what if there's an emergency?" Mr. Yao bellowed.

"Billy Bob and Mrs. T will be here," I said calmly. They'd kindly volunteered to keep an eye on the place at night and step in if there was ever a crisis. "Besides, we wouldn't be far away. All the houses we're looking at—they're only a ten-minute drive."

Mr. Yao shook his head firmly. "This is not gonna work. The whole point of me hiring you guys is so you can *be* here!"

Now it was my turn to frown.

"Well, we don't work for you anymore. We work for ourselves now."

Mr. Yao shook a finger at me. "This is my motel too!"

I was starting to get steaming hot arguing with him, so I turned and started for the door.

"Where you going?!" he demanded.

I ignored him and kept moving, even as the phone started to ring.

"Mia! The phone!" Mr. Yao cried.

"Answer it!" I called back. "I thought it was your motel too!"

As I reached the door, I heard Mr. Yao pick up the call. I giggled as he put on his sweetest customer service voice.

"Good afternoon! Calivista Motel. This is Michael Yao. How may I assist your call today?" he cooed.

I wished my Polaroid camera could record it. Mr. Yao had one of the softest, funniest customer service voices I'd ever heard. It was like listening to a polar bear sing a lullaby.

. . .

I found Jason scrambling to unpack all the new restaurant tables his dad had ordered.

"I don't know how we're gonna squeeze all these in," he said, wiping the sweat off his brow with a napkin. "It won't be the same experience! It'll be like trying to eat in line at Space Mountain!"

"So tell him you don't want to do it," I urged. "You like this place the way it is."

Jason stopped moving. We put a couple of menus down on the hot curb and sat on top of them.

"He'll never listen. You know he grew up in a restaurant? My grandfather owned a little Chinese place—over in San Gabriel Valley. He was like you, working the phones every day while his parents cooked."

I put a hand to my chest. "Mr. Yao was like *me*? I doubt it."

"Look! I found his old journal!"

"Where?" I asked.

"In the garage! When I was helping my mom clean up the leak."
Jason pulled out a little note from his back pocket. I unfolded it
and read.

Dear diary,
Today this guy left a double A battery in
the tip jar. Can you believe that? A battery!
I tried putting it in our clock and it didn't
even work.

"Mr. Yao had a tip jar?!" I shrieked.
Jason was smiling. "I know, right?? Keep reading!"
My eyes darted across the page.

Dad said we should be grateful the customers
leave us anything at all. In Taiwan, they don't
have tips.
    I don't know if he's saying that to make
me feel better, but we're Americans now.
Everything we do is American. So when the
customers walk by and ignore my jar, I feel
sad.
    I wish they could see how hard we
work. Dad's back hurts every night, and
Mom's fingers bleed from peeling and
deveining the shrimp all day. All I want is for
my parents to make a lot of money quickly
so we can go to Disneyland. Jeffrey in my

class says they have churros that smell like Mickey Mouse. I don't know what that's supposed to mean. But I hope someone will leave me a BIG tip so I can find out. The next time someone gives me a used battery as a tip, I am going to stick it in their soup.

Michael Yao

I stared at the words, disbelieving. Mr. Yao was *me*. All this time, I thought he was just a ruthless owner. But he had been through exactly what I had been through—my struggle was his struggle!

"Is there more?" I asked.

Jason shook his head. "I'll keep looking, though. There's tons of old boxes in our garage."

"I'll come help!" I volunteered. "Have you asked him about it?"

"God no. He never wants to talk about his childhood. He always changes the subject," Jason said. "It's like he has post-traumatic *restaurant* disorder."

I chuckled, the questions brewing in my mind. Did anyone ever give him a battery again? Did he ever go to Disneyland? I wished I could ask my former boss, along with the biggest question of all: If Mr. Yao used to be exactly like me, *what happened* to him?

"Hey, Dad!" Jason said then, and I looked up to see the grown-up version walking to our spot on the curb.

"I thought we'd go over the menu together for this week," Mr. Yao said, pointing to the menus under our butts and pulling out his reading glasses.

"Actually, Hank and I already did that," Jason said, getting up.

"You and Hank . . . I see." Mr. Yao frowned.

"But if you want, I can give you a sample tasting. You want to try this really great churro I made?"

"I hate churros," Mr. Yao snapped.

I scrambled to my feet. "But you haven't tried Jason's churro. It's literally out of this—" I started to say, but Jason cut me off.

"It's okay, Mia. If he doesn't want to try it, he doesn't want to try it," he muttered. Eyes down, he hurried to open the door to the restaurant. "I'll see you at home, Dad."

CHAPTER 12

At school the next day, I was still thinking about Mr. Yao's diary entry. I wished I could time-travel back to the '70s and go to his parents' restaurant. I'd help him out behind the cashier's desk, and I'd definitely leave them all a big tip. Maybe if people had treated young Michael Yao better, he would have treated us better when he grew up.

"You think the diary version of someone is the real version?" I asked Da-Shawn as we laid out the paper. We were in the newsroom, cutting out fonts and rearranging articles to make everything fit. The district couldn't afford the computer software to do it electronically, so we had to do everything by hand. Which took a *long* time.

"What do you mean?" Da-Shawn asked, picking up a *D* to add to the headline "Dear Future Me." It was a piece I'd been working on, a compilation of letters my classmates wrote to their future selves. Most of them were honest and authentic. Then there was Bethany:

> Dear future me,
> Smile because your teeth will finally be perfect.
> Use it to achieve all your dreams—you deserve
> it! Remember that life is a journey, don't

forget to stop and smell the flowers. Now and then you'll feel frustrated when something goes wrong. But remember, you got this! Always be nice to others. You never know if their parents might be important.

Love,
Bethany

"Do we have to publish this?" I asked Da-Shawn.

He took her piece and read it, chuckling. "Let's hope future Bethany finds another reason to be nice to someone!" He handed me the glue stick.

I frowned. I guess even Ms. Phony Flowers deserved to be published, but I wished she didn't have space on my page. I pasted Bethany's letter to our master sheet, trying to rub out the ink on *important* with my finger, until Da-Shawn gave me a look. *Fiiine.* I lifted my inky thumb.

"But this is so ridiculous," I protested. He knew as well as I did what Bethany's *really* like.

"You'd be surprised," Da-Shawn said. "Sometimes people's writing can be more revealing than anything else about them."

I raised an eyebrow. "You think so?"

Da-Shawn nodded.

"What if you read the diary of someone you thought you'd *never* have anything in common with . . . and it turned out, they were a lot like you?" I asked.

Da-Shawn looked over. "I'd be really excited!"

"But you can't talk about it with him," I added.

"Why not?"

I was pretty sure Mr. Yao would take me by my T-shirt and hang me off the pool fence if he knew I was reading his diaries.

"Because they're his *diaries*," I said. "They're supposed to be private."

"Maybe you can get him to talk about it some other way," Da-Shawn said.

"Like how?" I asked.

Da-Shawn thought for a second. "You could interview him for your column?"

I shook my head. Interview Mr. Yao? I was desperate for material, but not *that* desperate. "Nah," I said, then remembered to tell Da-Shawn about my plan. "But I do want to interview the Chinese women's soccer team!"

His editor eyes turned the size of marbles when he heard that. I grinned.

"That's a cover story right there!" he said, holding his hand up to give me a high five.

• • •

When I walked into PE, a couple kids asked when their "Dear Future Me" pieces were getting published.

"Next week!" I told them.

"Mine better be at the top," Bethany said as she showed off her latest Nikes to Joanne. "Check it out. These are the same sneakers that Mia wears!"

My ears perked up.

"Not you, Mia! Mia *Hamm*," she corrected. "Like I'd *ever* buy your shoes!"

My eyes plunged down to my Payless sneakers. They looked just like Nikes. They even had a little swoosh on them, in the form of a long kangaroo tail, which I'd thought was totally cute in the store. Now it just looked . . . like a tail.

I tripped over my laces, remembering how I'd worry and wonder when my mom would finally buy me jeans. But now I didn't have the right shoes. There was always something.

Jason rushed over to me. "Forget about it. You look great."

I gave him a half smile as I got back up.

Stuart hustled over to Joanne in his own Nikes. "Hey! You going to the World Cup?" he asked her. "My dad's going to try to get tickets!"

I looked at them, deeply jealous that they were getting tickets and I wasn't. All they were probably going to get out of the match was a longer shopping list at Big 5.

"I'd love to, but I'm not sure we can get the tickets."

"Maybe . . . you can go with us . . ." Stuart suggested.

I peeked over to see Stuart making heart eyes at Joanne. Was he asking what I thought he was asking? *Stuart?* The same guy who once caught a fly with his hand and chased all the girls around the room with his fist shouting, "Is there a fly in your hair?"

"I'd love that!" Joanne cooed.

"Great," Stuart exclaimed enthusiastically. "It's a date!"

Jason and I exchanged glances. I could see he was resisting the urge to gag too.

Stuart's eyes then darted worriedly to me. "You're not going to write about this, are you, Mia?"

I quickly shook my head and put up my hands. "No! You're good."

Stuart relaxed and told Joanne he'd call her.

As Mr. Antwell separated us into soccer teams, Joanne immediately ran to Bethany, the two of them giggling with delight over what just happened. Once again, I stood around like an old vacuum hose, waiting to be called. I thought of Lupe's words as I waited. Why did we all act so weird now that our bodies were changing?

I lifted my arm and sniffed my armpit. But it still didn't stink. I examined my wrist for arm hair. But it was still as bald as a cucumber.

Be patient, I told myself. I reminded myself that last year I liked Da-Shawn. That was proof that *my mind* was changing. It was only a matter of time before my body caught up.

I was so deep in thought, I didn't hear Mr. Antwell blow his whistle and call my name.

"Mia!" he was yelling. "The game started! You're on Jason's team! C'mon!"

I tossed a smile at my friend and looked down at the ball right by my feet. What's more, the goal was wide open. But as my classmates started coming toward me, I panicked. All I could think about was the impact of sixteen feet, all with fancier cleats than me, kicking at me, trying to get the ball. What if I got hurt? What if I had to go to the emergency room? *What if . . . what if . . . what if?*

Paralyzed with fear, my feet turned to Jell-O.

Mr. Antwell plunged his head to his clipboard, disappointed. As Bethany swooped in and stole the ball, several of my teammates banged their shoulders hard into me as they ran past. "Thanks *a lot*," they hissed.

No amount of *it's okay*'s from Jason made me feel better. I wanted to shrivel up and disappear into the grass.

• • •

After class, I walked up to Mr. Antwell. He was talking to Lucas about the World Cup.

"Let me tell you, it's gonna be one of the most exciting sporting events in recent history."

"In *history*?" Lucas asked, skeptical. "C'mon, it's *girls'* soccer."

"So?" I interjected.

"So girls are weaker," Lucas said. "That's why they have their own team."

"Lucas!" Mr. Antwell scowled.

"What? It's true!" Lucas protested. "Girls are so much wimpier—everyone knows that."

"Wimpier? Do you know how hard these women had to work to get to the World Cup?" I informed Lucas. "How many pounds of sweat they've shed just so girls in the future won't have to listen to you say that?"

That shut him up.

"All right, Mia!" Mr. Antwell's eyes sparkled. "I've never seen you so fired up before—especially about soccer!"

Lucas rolled his eyes and walked away.

"Actually . . . Mr. Antwell, there's something I wanted to ask you," I started to say. "I've been thinking a lot about the World Cup."

"That's great!" Mr. Antwell beamed, taking off his sunglasses.

"I'm thinking of writing about it." I launched into my plan to find and interview the Chinese players. As I talked his ear off, Mr. Antwell picked up the soccer cones from the field.

"Tell you what," he finally said. "If you can get an interview with the women's team—either team—I will change your grade for the class."

"You mean it??" I erupted.

"Has to be a *good* interview. A real sit-down, Oprah-style situation. Not just a hello and a Polaroid—that's not gonna cut it."

"Oh, don't you worry, Mr. Antwell, I'm a pro at what I do!" I started helping with the cones.

"This nut might be a hard one to crack, even for you. Those guys have more security than the queen of England!"

I raised a finger. "The queen of England doesn't know motels like the back of her hand!"

Mr. Antwell looked confused as I spelled out my strategy of visiting every single hotel and inn in Pasadena, and as backup, calling up Chinese restaurants and seeing if anybody had ordered twenty beef noodle soups.

"You know, if you put just an ounce of that determination into playing the sport, you could get an A the traditional way."

A smile escaped as I handed him the cones. "I've never done anything the traditional way," I said. "Besides, writing—well, it's kinda my sport. I'm gonna show you what I'm made of!"

Mr. Antwell smiled and nodded, and I ran off the field, legs fired up on the hope and excitement that I might still be able to go to journalism camp after all.

When I stopped at the water fountain, Joanne was still cooing to Bethany about Stuart.

"I can't believe he asked me out!" she gushed. "To the World Cup too! That's like the equivalent of two movies!"

I dabbed the water from my lips.

Bethany giggled, adding on another layer of Lip Smacker even though her lips already shone like two mirrors.

"You think China stands a chance?"

"No way. They're totally trash compared to us," Bethany said.

I looked away from Bethany's mirror lips, crouching down by the fountain to hide.

"Anyway, you gotta get Stuart to take you to the Pasadena Grill after. I was there with my dad this weekend. And they had this burger! It was crunchy, like someone put chips in there!"

I jumped up. "Did you say the Pasadena Grill?"

But the bell rang, and Bethany ran off without answering. I resisted the urge to bolt home to tell Hank that the Grill must have loved his recipe because they were serving up his burgers! He was going to lose his mind!

CHAPTER 13

"Hank!!!" I called as soon as I got home from school.

But Hank wasn't at the restaurant or at the desk. Maybe he was over at the Grill, signing his new contract!

Speaking of Pasadena, I picked up the phone and started calling Chinese noodle shops in the area. I dialed up ten restaurants, but none of the owners said they had received a large food order delivered to a hotel.

"Are you sure?" I asked over and over. Where were the soccer players getting their fix? I knew whenever I ate American food three days in a row, I *needed* my mother's tomato and egg noodles.

"Yes," one owner said sadly. "Business been down seventy percent since the soccer fever started."

"Really?" I asked, surprised.

"Anytime people have to pick sides, USA or China, we caught in the middle. Not easy."

I thought again of my two sides. I wanted to think they were two liquids mixing nicely, like boba milk tea. But some days they felt more like two glass plates, rubbing against each other and cracking.

With a sigh, the restaurant owner told me that some of their regulars had canceled reservations. "We thinking of closing on the big day, in case Team China wins and there are riots," he said. "You never know in this country."

It hurt my heart. "But still, the fact that they made it this far . . ." I said in a small voice.

"Oh, yes," he admitted. "As a Chinese person, I'm proud."

I smiled.

"If you do meet the Chinese women," the owner added, "tell them good luck."

"I will! Call me if you hear anything," I said. "I'm at the Calivista Motel."

Hank's car pulled in as I hung up the phone.

I jumped off the stool and ran outside to him. "Hank!!! When were you gonna tell me the Grill's using your recipe? Congratulations!!!"

Hank looked at me, confused. "What do you mean? They never called me."

"They didn't?" I asked. "So you weren't there signing the contract just now?"

"No. I was at the store," Hank said, holding up some ground beef from Ralphs.

"But Bethany said she ate your burger there this weekend."

Hank dropped the bag and headed for the front office. Hurriedly, Hank grabbed the phone, punching in the number for the restaurant, his face brimming with excitement. "Roger must have really loved it! This is it! My big break!"

Mr. Yao walked in as Hank was dialing. "What's the big fuss about?" he asked.

Hank hung up. "I'm cooking up a real important deal with the Pasadena Grill."

"Now you're thinking of leaving too?"

Hank looked at Mr. Yao, amused.

Mr. Yao fumbled while Hank crossed his arms. Though it had been years, he'd still never apologized to Hank for falsely accusing him of stealing a customer's car and kicking him out of the motel.

"Thought you didn't want me here," Hank added.

"That was *before*," Mr. Yao said by way of explanation. "When I didn't really know you." He looked down, and it seemed to be a real effort for him to add, "What would happen to East Meets West if you left? Jason would be devastated."

"Ohhhhhh, so it was okay *then* to treat me like trash," Hank said, "before you realized you needed me." I felt the room go still. I gazed at Mr. Yao, then at Hank. I was so proud of him for finally having this conversation, for not letting Mr. Yao off the hook after all these years. The pain of racism was like a cavity—it chipped away until we addressed it.

"Why do you have to go dredging up the past?"

"Because the past, believe it or not, stays with us, until it's made right."

Mr. Yao didn't say anything. He was too proud to admit the error of his ways, but also too smart now to offend Hank.

"I'm sorry," Mr. Yao finally said.

Hank thought long and hard.

"That's a start," he said. "I'm also going to need you to back off with the tables. This isn't a bus terminal. We're not squeezing as many people in as we can."

Mr. Yao pushed out the word "Fine."

Hank smiled. "Good. Now if you'll excuse me, I have to call up my business partners, get my cut!"

As Hank disappeared into the manager's quarters to call the Grill, I gazed over at Mr. Yao. He was counting up the cash in our register, punching the amounts into a calculator with his finger. I wondered if his apology to Hank made him feel infinitely lighter.

There was still a scowl on his face. I tried to imagine him as a boy, not frowning.

"Stop looking at me like that."

"Like what?"

"Like you're watching a movie of me in your head and I'm not being played by someone good."

I stifled a laugh as I reached over for one of the mint candies at the front desk.

"I'm not!" I promised.

He went back to counting the cash. "You guys make an offer on the house yet?"

I shook my head, sucking on the mint. "My dad's trying to find an agent to show us more places. But it's hard." I thought about what Da-Shawn said, then cocked my head and took a chance. "Hey, Mr. Yao, do you remember when you were my age? Did you also work with your parents?"

He nodded. "That was a long time ago."

"Did you have friends like I have Jason and Lupe? Did the other kids at school know about your job?"

He frowned and banged the cash register closed. "Why are you asking me all these personal questions?"

I bit my lip, fighting the urge to tell him that I had spent all night creating five different versions of his childhood in my head. I wanted to see which one I'd gotten right. "Just curious . . ."

Jason walked in from the back to get some more dollar bills for change at the restaurant. "What are you guys talking about?" he asked.

"Your dad's childhood."

Jason grabbed his stool. "So what happened?"

"Nothing happened!" Mr. Yao insisted. "I worked. Then I grew up. Then I worked some more—end of story."

"That's not what you wrote about in—" Jason started to say.

"You've been spending too much time in that garage," Mr. Yao snapped. "Soon as your mother fixes the leak, all those boxes are going! I'm going to clear out all the junk!"

"No!" Jason protested. "I need to find my grandparents' recipes!"

"Stop looking to the past to help you," Mr. Yao scolded. "You gotta make your own way, son."

Jason stared down at his shoelaces. I offered him a mint, but he shook his head.

Hank walked in from the manager's quarters and grabbed his car keys. "They're still not answering the phone at the Grill," he said. "I'm gonna go up there before the dinner rush."

I grabbed my reporter's notebook and pen. "Good idea! Maybe we can stop by a few more hotels on the way home? I've already called all the Chinese restaurants. No luck."

"Can I come too?" Jason asked, perking up.

"What about our restaurant?!" Mr. Yao said as we both hopped off our stools.

"Relax! Our first reservation's not for hours," Hank told him.

"So who's going to man the front desk?"

"You can!" I told him. Smiling, I took a piece of paper and made a little sign, remembering my first day at the motel. *Michael Yao, Assistant Manager*, I scribbled. Now that I'd read Mr. Yao's journal, I was confident he could handle the job.

His jaw dropped at the sign. *"Assistant?!"*

"Hey, you gotta start somewhere!" I grinned and followed Jason and Hank out the door.

CHAPTER 14

"Why does he always have to put me down?" Jason said once we were in the car on our way to Pasadena. "And now I can't even escape to the Calivista because he just follows me here."

I sighed. It must be so hard.

But I also thought of Mr. Yao asking Hank to stay, even when it was obvious he was jealous of him spending so much time with Jason. He saw how much his son needed Hank. That was progress.

I told Jason about it.

"That's good," Jason said. "Still, I wish he could be nicer to me. He seemed so nice in that diary entry."

"Have you asked your mom about his childhood?" I asked.

"She says she doesn't know much. She didn't even get to meet my grandparents," he added with a sigh. "Both my agong and ama died before I was born."

I put a hand on Jason's shoulder. "I'm so sorry." I couldn't imagine losing my own grandparents, even though they were back in China. It felt like yesterday that I last saw them, even though it was last Christmas. My heart ached for them.

Jason reached up and patted my fingers. "Thanks. Oh, and here." Digging into his pocket, Jason handed me a piece of yellowed paper.

"Another note!" I exclaimed.

"I found it cleaning out one of the boxes," Jason said. "I haven't read it yet."

We opened it together.

Dear diary,

Dad's back is done busted. I blame the hot chili oyster sauce he insisted on making from scratch. He spent HOURS in front of the stove. Now look at him. Can't even sit down.

I told him he should have just bought the stuff at the store. Who cares if it tastes different? Americans don't know! Most of the people who come through, all they want is orange chicken. They don't even care what it tastes like. They just like the color. It's like eating a highlighter.

But Dad said he cares. He knows the difference.

Now he can't move and I'm stuck helping Mom make highlighter chicken. My eyes hurt from mincing the ginger root. One time Mom put some in my lunch box. The other kids wouldn't stop laughing for a week—look, Michael's eating a potato with fingers!

Now I check my lunch box every day. If there's something weird in there, I swap it for some Lay's chips.

When I grow up, I'm not gonna eat

highlighter chicken. I'm not gonna be like Mom and Dad and work all the time. I'm gonna actually ENJOY MY LIFE.

Michael Yao

Jason put the note down.

"Are you sure your *dad* wrote this?" I asked. The same guy who built the manager's quarters right behind the front office so we could work *while* we slept? The guy who didn't believe in taking a single day off, not even at Christmas? *He* just wanted to "enjoy life"?!

Jason pointed at the handwriting, which made a little loop at the *T*. "That's him."

I nodded, still remembering Mr. Yao's many Post-it scribbles— *Don't Waste Towels!!! No long hot showers!!! The pool is for customers ONLY!*

"Maybe in college, he decided he wanted to work really, really hard?" Jason guessed.

"More like work others really hard," I muttered. I glanced back at the note. "Are you sure we should keep reading these? I mean, they're personal."

"If he wanted us to stop reading, he would have moved the boxes ages ago," Jason said. "Besides, aren't they fascinating?"

"Fascinating for you." I didn't know how to tell Jason, but it kind of hurt that Mr. Yao had worked my parents so hard, now that I knew that he knew *exactly* what that felt like.

Hank turned the radio down and glanced at us in the mirror.

"What are you two bickering about?" he asked.

Jason held up the entry.

"What's that?" Hank asked.

"My dad's diary!"

Hank nearly turned off the wrong exit. "No way! Spill the beans—what was he like??"

"He was shockingly great!" I all but shouted, still confused. "Like totally funny and everything!"

Jason read the part about the orange chicken to Hank.

"That's hysterical." Hank chortled with laughter. "I love orange chicken. That's always the first thing I order."

"But I'm confused. Why'd he treat us that way if he knew what it's like to be in our shoes?" I asked.

Hank sucked in a deep breath as he pulled off the freeway to Pasadena. "People are complicated," he said. "But the fact that he *used* to be so kind gives me hope." Hank smiled at me in the rearview mirror. "Proves it's in there, like a good marinade. Just takes a little more time to grill. Speaking of the Grill, you guys ready?"

I looked up at the Pasadena Grill sign.

As Hank and Jason got out of the car, I stayed behind an extra second. I knew if I wanted to be a journalist, I had to put my biases behind me. But was I ready to find out the real deal with Mr. Yao's past?

CHAPTER 15

Jason stared at the white tablecloths and waiters in suits at the Grill. "Now, this is a classy restaurant!" he said as I ran up to him and Hank.

He bolted inside the dining room before the hostess could stop him, checking out the different silverware and using his arms to measure the space between tables. I spotted a large *GO, TEAM USA!* sign hanging on a far wall. My American side smiled inside.

Hank turned to the hostess.

"Is Roger around?" he asked her. "Tell him Hank's here to see him."

"Do you have an appointment?" she asked.

"No, but he'll know who I am." Hank picked up a menu as we waited. "Look at that!" He held it up proudly.

There, in big bold letters, were the words: *Crunch Burger—New!*

The hostess put the phone down. "I'm sorry, but Mr. Wamble is unavailable."

"Did you tell him Hank's here?"

"He said he didn't know any Hank."

"There's gotta be a mistake. Try him again!"

The hostess looked uneasy as she reached for the phone again. This time, Hank took the receiver from her.

"Wamble, it's Hank Caleb. Cut the mustard—what's going on here? You're not gonna see me? I'm *on the menu*!"

Hank waited a moment, then hung up and started marching toward Mr. Wamble's office.

The hostess tried to stop him. "No! Wait—"

But Hank just kept walking through the dining room, grabbing as many menus out of people's hands as he could along the way. I scrambled to keep up and tried to get Jason's attention at the same time, but he seemed to be sampling home-whipped butter and popovers on the other side of the room.

We found Mr. Wamble at his desk balancing a fork on his lip when we walked in. The fork crashed onto his table. "I already told you, I'm late for a meeting, I can't talk right now."

"You're not going anywhere until you explain what's going on," Hank said. He dumped the tower of menus onto Mr. Wamble's desk. They landed with a thud. "You mind telling me why my recipe's in there without proper compensation?"

"This isn't your recipe!" Mr. Wamble replied.

"Of course it's Hank's!" I blurted. "We were here the other day. You even said, 'I can see why so many people like it! The crunch! The texture!'—those were your *exact words*!"

Hank pointed at me. "See here? I have a witness!"

"So yours had a little crunch too," said Mr. Wamble. "Big deal. So do a lot of sandwiches. That's just a mere coincidence."

"A mere coincidence?!" Hank grabbed his hair. His lips were trembling; he could hardly speak.

"The recipe Hank left with you guys—did you make it or not?" I asked Mr. Wamble point-blank.

"Yes, we did."

"And?"

"Not bad," he said. "A little salty, but overall, a pretty decent burger. But hardly spectacular. So we did a little improvising and we made it our own."

Hank pointed to him, sitting there in his expensive leather chair. "You stole, is what you did."

"We didn't steal anything," Mr. Wamble said with a huff. "You'll find that our Crunch Burger is made of wagyu beef, and that's not in your recipe."

"Just putting in a fancier beef doesn't make it yours—"

"And instead of plain saltine crackers, we're using rosemary-oil-infused sourdough crackers," he continued.

"Oh, *rosemary*-infused!" Hank mocked.

"*And* we're using persimmon ketchup."

"I don't care what kind of Mickey Mouse ketchup you use, you're still putting crackers in the burgers—that's *my* idea!"

"Ideas are not copyrighted, my friend," Mr. Wamble said with a little smile.

"Sure they are! It took me years to come up with that recipe. It was my life's work! And you just took it!"

Mr. Wamble snorted. "If that's your life's work, then it's a sorry little life."

Hank's jaw dropped. I grabbed his hand. I wasn't about to let this burger thief talk to him that way.

"You'll be sorry, Mr. Wamble," I said to him. "We'll be back—soon!"

"With a legal team!" Hank shouted as we walked out.

Anger thudded inside my chest as I crossed the dining room trying to find Jason. I thought of how excited Hank was just last week, his eyes full of hope as he marveled at the chandeliers. Now all the crystals were crashing down, slicing into him. This place was nothing more than a crooked cave filled with dumpster juice.

"Jason! C'mon, let's go!" I called.

"Mia! Hank! Look how cool this place is—they have caviar spoons made of pearl!" Jason gushed.

"I don't want to hear it," I said, taking him by the elbow and leading him out. Hank had already gone to the car, and besides, it didn't matter how impressive and fancy-looking the Grill was—we were out of there! I dragged him to the parking lot.

"*And* the coach of the US women's soccer team was just in here!" he said, pulling his arm free.

That got my attention. I stopped walking.

CHAPTER 16

"Are you sure?" I said. "The US coach was just here?"

Jason pointed to a black van parked across the Grill's lot.

"He's in there right now, with twenty Crunch Burgers!" Jason said.

"*Twenty* Crunch Burgers?!"

My mind was racing. That many burgers could only mean one thing—the players must be in the van too! I ran the rest of the way to Hank's car.

"Hank! We'll be right back!" I said breathlessly. "The US women's soccer team! They're eating your burgers!"

Despite the unspeakable way he'd just been treated, Hank still managed a smile. "Wow. You better go get your interview!" he urged. "What are you still standing there for?"

Heart hammering, I grabbed my reporter's notebook from the back seat.

"C'mon," I told Jason.

We walked toward the black van. My nerves were jangling. This was the *US women's soccer team*! The people sitting inside were billboard people!

I could tell Jason was nervous too. He kept breathing into his hand to see if his breath stank.

"How do I look?" he asked, combing his fingers through his hair.

"Ummmm . . . it's an interview, not a date," I reminded him.

"Hey, you *never* know," he said. I frowned at Jason as he spat into his palm and patted his hair.

Gently, we knocked on the driver's side window. The dark glass rolled down an inch.

"Can we help you?"

I couldn't see inside at all because the window was tinted so thoroughly. It sounded like a man, and I pictured the coach, snarfing down a burger as he went over strategy with Briana Scurry, Brandi Chastain, and Mia Hamm. At the thought of Mia, I stepped on my tippy-toes. Was she in there too?

"My name is Mia Tang, and I'm a student journalist. This is my assistant, Jason."

"Colleague," Jason corrected. "And we're huge fans. We were wondering, could we get like an autograph or something?"

I heard whispers inside.

Then, suddenly, the back door opened, and we were face-to-face with the biggest women's soccer stars on the planet.

Jason looked a little light-headed, and I grabbed his arm just in case as the team blinded us with their bright smiles and even brighter jerseys. I let out a squeal of excitement as Mia, Briana, and Brandi whipped out permanent markers and started signing our T-shirts.

Jason held out his arm and pleaded, "Can you sign that too?"

And they obliged. They were genuinely the nicest people ever.

I grabbed my Polaroid and started snapping pictures as Jason jotted the address of the Calivista on a blank page in my reporter's notebook and handed it to goalkeeper Briana Scurry.

"This is our restaurant! We'd love to have you guys over—anytime! On the house!" he said. "I make the best shrimp-mango dumplings!"

"Shrimp-mango dumplings?" Briana asked Mia. "We've never had that before, have we?"

I turned to Mia Hamm and said, "My name's Mia too. And I'm a student reporter. May I ask you some questions?"

"Mia! How great to meet you," she said with a big smile. "We're not doing any press at the moment. But I can take a picture with you—how about that?"

I nodded excitedly, trying not to think of Mr. Antwell's warning: *No Polaroids, that's not gonna cut it.* But a Polaroid with Mia Hamm *had* to be worth a thousand words!

As Mia put her arm around me and we both smiled at the camera, she asked if I played soccer.

I shook my head.

"Well, if you ever decide to, it's pretty great," she said.

"The most fun you'll ever have!" Briana added.

"I'm not that athletic," I said shyly.

"You don't have to be super athletic to enjoy sports," Mia said. "Just play for the fun of it!"

Briana started demonstrating, jumping around the lot, dribbling a permanent marker with her feet. I laughed. Funny how, if you replaced the ball with a pen, it looked like much more fun to me.

"Can I try?" I asked.

Briana grinned, and "passed" the permanent marker to me. I kicked it to Mia, who kicked it back to Briana. "Teamwork makes the dream work!" Briana shouted.

"And what a dream!" Mia shouted. Then she leaned over to me and added, "We made it to the World Cup! Can you believe it? Just goes to show, anything's possible if you dream big and work hard!"

I suddenly wished so hard that Lupe could've been there.

Then Mia Hamm signed the Polaroid of the two of us *To Mia, from Mia*, and I hugged it to my chest. I wanted to tell her that for the first time, all the pieces of me were playing together. Instead, I said, "Thanks, Mia, I hope you guys kill it out there!"

She winked at me. "For girls like you!"

With that, they jumped back into the van and hit the road. I waved and smiled so hard, my face hurt. Right then, I thought, it didn't really matter who won. The fact that we got here, it made my heart sing.

CHAPTER 17

We rode the high from seeing Team USA all the way home. It didn't matter that the three hotels we stopped at along the way didn't have the Chinese players. All that mattered was we had gotten to meet Mia Hamm!

"Dad!!! Guess what??" Jason said when we got back, as Hank went to search for Mrs. T. He was going to look up what Mr. Wamble said in one of Mrs. T's big books on the law.

"Just a minute," Mr. Yao said. He was wagging his finger at my mom as she pushed a big whiteboard out of the manager's quarters.

"Where are you going with that thing?" Mr. Yao asked.

"I'm moving it to my room so I can teach these kids," Mom answered. Mom had gotten the board at a yard sale the other week. I rushed over to help her.

"Teach what kids?" Mr. Yao peered inside the guest room where my mom had been staying. There were a bunch of Math Cup kids inside, including Lupe. She was right—they were all boys except for her. I recognized Ethan right away, the one with the dimples who everyone thought was cute. Lupe was sitting as far from him as she could, her eyes glued to her book. There was no way she liked him. "What is this??" Mr. Yao asked.

"Math Cup!" Mom said. "You know I teach math at the high

school now. Well, these kids are competing in a math competition, and their coach, well, he's more interested in *saying* he coaches them than actually coaching."

"Wait, what did the administration say?" I asked Mom.

"They said Mr. Jammer's the official coach and wouldn't let me take over." Mom stuck out her lower lip, sad. "They said I'd be stepping on Mr. Jammer's toes."

"His toes are hardly ever in the classroom!" one of the boys hollered.

"Exactly. Which is why I'm gonna teach you here," Mom said.

Lupe threw up her arms and cheered.

"But does it have to be *here*?" Mr. Yao asked. "In the motel?"

"Technically, this is my bedroom," Mom reminded him.

Mr. Yao started pulling the whiteboard back out. "We need these rooms for paying guests! Tell them they gotta go home. This is a business, not a school!"

Mom looked at her students, hesitating.

"What next? We're gonna start offering haircuts here too?" Mr. Yao continued. He pointed at the kids. "Out!"

"Just a minute!" Panicking, Mom reached into her purse and pulled out a fifty-dollar bill. She thrust it at Mr. Yao, her chest rising and falling. "There, you happy now? I'm a paying customer!"

I glared at Mr. Yao as he stuffed the money into his pocket. "Thank you," he said, returning the whiteboard to her. "Don't forget. Checkout is at eleven."

Mom slammed the door in his face.

As Mr. Yao walked back to the front office with my mom's money, I trailed after him.

"Why'd you have to do that?" I asked, my nostrils flaring. "You're such a grouch!"

"Someone's gotta maintain order in this jungle," he said, pushing open the door to the front office.

"No," I fumed as he added Mom's fifty dollars to the cash register. "You just enjoy pushing people around." I narrowed my eyes at him. *"Why?"*

Jason interrupted before he could answer, though, and as he told his dad all about meeting Mia Hamm, I reached in and grabbed my mom's fifty dollars back. No way was my mom paying to stay at her own motel. I put it in my pocket.

"That's great! What'd they say when you invited them?" Mr. Yao said, not grumpy anymore. "Are they coming to the Calivista for dinner?"

"I think so, right, Mia?"

I nodded enthusiastically. "They were so nice!"

"They said they'd never had shrimp-mango dumplings before!" Jason added.

Mr. Yao's eyebrows knitted. "You told them you make shrimp-mango dumplings? Why'd you tell them that?"

"Uhhh, because we do?" Jason replied.

"You should have said something more American," Mr. Yao lamented. "Anything!"

I wanted to shout his own words at him: *We're Americans now. Everything we do is American.* But knowing Mr. Yao, he'd probably charge me a fee for reading his diary.

"They're going to love my dumplings," Jason muttered. "You'll see."

"Are you *sure* they're coming?" Mr. Yao asked.

Jason mustered up every confidence and told his dad it was definitely happening.

"Then we have to go shopping! Make this place look like a five-star restaurant. I'm talking flowers. Rugs. Those fancy soaps that smell so good, you want to eat them. Jason, you're coming with me to Home Depot."

Jason gazed in the direction of the kitchen. "I'd better stay here and get ready for the dinner rush. Hank's still in Mrs. T's room, looking at legal stuff."

Mr. Yao let out a sigh of disappointment. He turned to me. "Then, Mia, you come with me. I'll get you a Slurpee along the way."

I threw a hand to my chest. "Me?" I asked. Was Mr. Yao really suggesting what I thought he was suggesting?

"Let's go shopping!"

CHAPTER 18

"Can I get a large Slurpee?" I asked Mr. Yao when we got to the 7-Eleven.

"Let's make it a small," he answered.

I reached for the cup and filled it all the way. A small Slurpee was still bigger than anything Mr. Yao had gotten me before.

I sipped my drink as we drove Coast Boulevard, gazing at the small jade sculpture of an ox hanging from Mr. Yao's car mirror. It was weird being inside his giant Navigator. I'd spent years sitting at the desk, scanning the streets for it, tensing up whenever I saw it. But I'd never made it inside.

I pointed to the ox. "Is that a good-luck charm?"

My parents hung all sorts of Chinese charms in our car too—there was a cat for long life, a fish for luck, a coin for prosperity, and bamboo to remind us to always be strong but kind. Glancing at Mr. Yao's mirror, I would have thought he'd have a lot more coins.

"Never mind about my charm," he said. He pointed to my reporter's notebook, which I'd brought along. "Make a list in that notebook of yours. We need new tablecloths, napkins, those little tabletop sets where you can take itty-bitty sandwiches off them . . ."

He pinched his fingers together, mimicking Alice in Wonderland, and I almost burst out laughing.

"Okay." I scribbled everything down.

"Oh, and a champagne bucket. They're going to want some champagne after they win. Make that two!"

"But, Mr. Yao, what if they don't win?"

"Let me tell you something. Sports is like a business. Whoever has more money's gonna win. They'll have better coaches, better equipment, better everything. The little guys won't stand a chance. That's just how it is in life."

"You're forgetting about passion."

Mr. Yao's face tightened. "Passion's the most dangerous ingredient of all."

"Why?"

"Because it can lead you to make mistakes. You stop thinking straight. You keep going, and going, even when you should have stopped a long time ago."

"Yeah, and then you break through!" I said. "That's how we bought the motel from you. You weren't budging, and we were so tempted to give up. But we didn't. We kept going and going until we finally got it!"

I threw my arms up so triumphantly, my hands hit the roof. *Owww.*

Mr. Yao frowned at me. "That was a rare exception. But *most* of the time, that kind of story is just a fantasy ride at Disneyland."

For someone whose own life resembled a fantasy ride—here he was, the owner of *multiple* motels, and now a restaurant—he sure sounded pessimistic.

"Is that what happened in your life?"

He wriggled in his seat.

"It's just . . . you own a lot of properties, but you never really seem happy."

"I'm happy!" he practically shouted. "Whenever we make a lot of money, I'm happy."

"Are you? Usually, you just take the envelope and you go, 'It better all be in there,'" I said in my best Mr. Yao voice. "You never say, 'Keep up the good work.' Or 'Go, team!'"

He gave me a look. "You want me to say 'Go, team'?"

This time, I had to laugh. "Once in a while, yeah," I said.

Mr. Yao shook his head. "My father didn't believe in empty praise."

I sat up, eager for more details. "He was a chef, right?" I asked, writing in my notebook. "Jason told me."

Mr. Yao nodded. "He was a lot of things."

"Was it hard always having to do your homework in the kitchen? Did the other kids know? Did you learn to make other dishes, besides highlighter chicken?" I asked him. *Oops.* I'd meant to ask just one question.

Mr. Yao chuckled and looked at me, surprised. "You call it highlighter chicken too? I could never understand why it was so popular."

"Do you miss it?" I asked, relieved that he didn't realize I'd quoted his own diary entry. "Cooking in the kitchen with your parents?"

He thought long and hard. "No," he finally said. "But I do miss them."

I put my notebook down. He suddenly looked so alone and lost in thought, I felt sad for him. It was weird to see Mr. Yao so vulnerable. I wanted to reach out with a blanket and cover him.

"How did they pass away?" I asked after a moment.

He shook his head.

"Did they get to see the Calivista, at least?"

He just stared ahead, pretending like he didn't hear me.

"I bet if they were alive, they'd be proud of you," I offered. Mr. Yao glanced over, as surprised as I was to hear my words. But everyone was someone's child, even Mr. Yao.

"I doubt it," he muttered. Before I could ask him anything else, he turned into the Home Depot lot. "You ready for a restaurant shopping spree?"

I definitely was.

CHAPTER 19

Mr. Yao was like a vacuum cleaner, spinning through Home Depot, gobbling up everything in sight. We bought plates, glasses, white linen tablecloths, flowers, vases, throw rugs, and candles. You name it, we bought it. And when it came time to pay, he didn't even blink.

"That'll be $875.29," the cashier said.

Mr. Yao handed over his platinum Visa card like it was all free. Just a few years ago, he would have bitten my head off if we spent eight dollars. Now he happily loaded up on expensive decor, no questions asked. I guess when it came to his son's dream, no amount was too high.

"I can't believe we bought all this," I chuckled as we loaded everything into the car.

Mr. Yao carefully arranged the fragile plates and closed the trunk. "I just don't want him to fail," he said quietly.

"Jason? He won't," I assured him. "His food's amazing."

"Life's not a meritocracy, Mia. You of all people should know that."

I thought about that statement the rest of the way home. I wasn't sure I agreed with Mr. Yao, especially about America. Sure, I'd witnessed plenty of times when people with more money, more opportunities, or sometimes simply a different color skin got ahead. Just today, Hank's life's work was ripped off in broad daylight and the guy didn't even say sorry!

But still, I wanted to believe that life *was* a meritocracy. That if someone dreamed big, worked hard, and tried with everything they had, they could achieve anything. The upcoming women's soccer match was a testament to that.

We were both quiet on the drive back. Mr. Yao kept his eyes straight ahead, glued to the goal that if he threw enough money at the restaurant, Jason wouldn't let him down.

. . .

Back at the Calivista, Jason helped his dad unload the Navigator, and I found Hank. He was at the front desk, on the phone.

"Thanks for your advice," Hank said. "I'll see you in your office in Orange."

"What's going on?" I asked after he hung up.

"I'm getting myself a lawyer. Wamble's not going to get away with this."

"Good for you!"

As Hank turned back to the phone, I went to find my mom. She was in her room, wiping the whiteboard.

"Oh, good, you're back," she said.

I dug into my pocket and handed my mom's fifty dollars back to her. She gave me a grateful smile.

"Can you believe the nerve of that man?" she asked. "The way he talks to us, it's like we're still his employees. We've *got* to get a place of our own!"

I nodded, feeling her anxiety and hearing the whimpers of

my future puppy. In my head, I'd already named him Comma.

"Oh! Your dad said he might have found an agent."

"Really?"

"Yeah! And he has a good listing for us. Tomorrow after school, we'll go," Mom said.

I grinned. I hoped this place didn't have a hole in the roof. Or if it did, that it was smaller.

"How'd the Math Cup meeting go?" I asked.

Mom sighed. "The kids are rusty in a lot of areas. We'll need to practice every day to get them up to speed. Otherwise they'll never be ready for the first competition."

"If anyone can get them ready, it's you," I reminded her.

"But I can't have Mr. Yao interrupting my classes and giving me a hard time! That was so humiliating! It's bad enough they won't let me coach them at the high school," Mom said. Biting her lip, she added, "The administration doesn't think my English is good enough to take them to the competitions. That's why I can't be their coach."

"What?!" I shrieked.

She looked down. "I know."

"That's absurd! You're a math teacher, not an English teacher!"

"I know. But I just started full-time, and I don't want to make any trouble. I'm just going to show them what I can do. Quietly."

I sighed. My parents were always trying to get things *quietly*. We'd been in the country for five years already. When could we actually start getting things *loudly*?

"I just need a few more sessions with the team," Mom said.

"I'll talk to Mr. Yao about meeting here."

"He'll never listen. It's *Mr. Yao*!"

But young Michael might. I'd caught a tiny glimpse of him in the car today. I knew he was still in there. I just had to find a way to get through to him.

CHAPTER 20

At school, Jason asked if I wanted to come over to his house. "Help me find more diary entries in the garage before my dad throws everything out?"

"Sure!"

A couple of girls walked by wearing soccer jerseys. More and more, kids were wearing World Cup gear around, and not just for PE. I'd been thinking about getting a jersey myself, except they were forty-nine dollars plus tax.

Jason ran over to the girls and held out the Polaroid of us and Mia Hamm. "Check it!" he said, grinning.

I chuckled.

"Oh my God!" they squealed. "What was she like? Tell us everything!"

"She was amazing! And she's coming over to my restaurant later!" he bragged. Then Jason turned to me, slightly worried. "She's gonna come, right? My dad sure bought a whole lot of flowers."

"Relax, they're coming," I said.

The girls told Jason to keep them posted, and he gave them each a card to East Meets West, trying to play it cool. I knew he was bubbling with excitement inside. After they left, he put the Polaroid away.

"So how was the shopping trip?" he asked me. "Did my dad say anything about me and the restaurant?"

I thought about Mr. Yao's words—*I just don't want him to fail*—and shook my head. "No, we just talked. He told me he missed his parents."

Jason's mouth turned into an O. "He said that?! That's more than I've ever heard about them!"

Mr. Antwell strolled down the hall, and I got temporarily distracted. "Mr. Antwell!" I called out. "Guess who we met yesterday? The US women's soccer team!"

"No kidding!" he said, walking over to me and Jason.

"Just outside the Pasadena Grill!" I reached out and Jason handed me the Polaroid.

"So did you interview them? Ask them questions about their journey to soccer stardom?" Mr. Antwell asked.

"No," I confessed. I presented him with the photo. "But I did get this!"

Mr. Antwell whistled. "Wow. Keep that—it'll be worth big money after the match!"

I smiled and tucked the Polaroid carefully into my back pocket. "So will you change my grade?" I asked hopefully.

Mr. Antwell shook his head with a sigh. "Afraid not. A deal's a deal. A Polaroid's not the same as an interview."

"But—"

"Sorry, Mia, I can't change your grade just because you spotted a celebrity."

"But they said they weren't taking any press!"

"You're just gonna have to figure something else out."

"I've already been to four hotels and I've called up every single Chinese restaurant in Pasadena, and I can't find the Chinese team! I don't know what else to do short of breaking into the Rose Bowl. And I'm sure that place is guarded like Fort Knox!"

"Where there's a will, there's a way," Mr. Antwell said, something I already knew well.

As I watched him walk away, I was starting to think it might be easier to get an A by actually kicking the ball.

· · ·

Later, after school, I waited for my parents to come home, kicking a pen with my feet in the parking lot. Dad was at the bank, and Mom was still at the high school. Hank was out meeting with lawyers, and Jason had to stay at school to work on a group project. So it was just me and Lupe minding the motel.

Lupe was taking my picture for the school paper. Unlike Mr. Antwell, Da-Shawn was stoked by the Mia Hamm Polaroid. We were publishing it, along with accounts from me and Jason.

Lupe brought over a soccer ball for the photo op. Still, I preferred kicking the pen.

"How was the Math Cup meeting today?" I asked.

"We *were* starting to get the hang of it, but then this girl Allie joined. She's a freshman."

"That's great! So you're not the only girl anymore?" I said, dribbling the pen.

"Nope! Except now all the boys are really distracted. They're too busy blushing and acting weird around her. She's really pretty."

I stopped kicking and looked over at Lupe. "How do you know she's pretty?"

Lupe shrugged. "She just is."

"But like, who decides?"

"I dunno," Lupe admitted. "The world, I guess."

The two of us studied our reflections in a guest room window. I reached out and patted my wild nest of hair. "You think we'll ever be pretty?"

Lupe thought about it. "Maybe," she finally said. "To sophisticated people, you know, who don't really care about that kind of stuff."

"Totally."

We sat down on the ground, leaning against the motel wall. "Do you ever worry about not growing up?"

Lupe gave me a funny look.

"Like, what if this is it? And I'll always look like a kid?" I asked, glancing down at my body.

Lupe chuckled. "You won't! What do you want, wrinkles on your neck?"

She grabbed the pen from the ground and pretended to try to draw on my neck. I shrieked with laughter, dodging her.

"No! But I want something! Even Jason has hairy legs now. I looked the other day, when we were in the car together."

"Trust me," Lupe said, "you don't want hairy legs like Jason's."

"Why not?" I asked. I didn't understand all these American rules. Like why did so many women shave their legs? It always clogged up our bathtubs, and my dad had to work hard to get it out.

"I dunno. Those are just the rules in this country for girls, I guess. No hairy legs. No stinky pits. Oh, and no unibrows."

"Unibrows?!" I quickly raised my hand to feel if there was any fuzz between my eyebrows. There wasn't. Phew. I turned to Lupe. "What about the rules for boys?"

She pondered for a while but finally shook her head. "I don't think they have any."

"That's not fair!"

"That's why I'm not going to shave," she said. "If I have hairy legs, I'm just going to leave them. And if I grow a unibrow, then I'll just be a unibrow queen!"

I giggled. "Me too!"

Lupe smiled.

It made me feel so much better that I had a friend I could talk to about these things.

Lupe got up and held out a hand, pulling me to my feet.

As I started kicking the pen on the ground again, Lupe reached over for her soccer ball and put it down in front of me.

"What are you doing?" I asked.

"Just pretend it's a pen," she urged. "C'mon. I need a photo of you kicking a ball!"

I stared at it. "I can't, okay?"

"What's the matter?"

I sighed heavily, then dropped down again, this time sitting on the ball.

"Are you worried about getting injured?" Lupe guessed. "Because we have insurance now . . ."

I looked away, biting on my lip. But the worry was as big as a billboard in my mind. "What's the point of trying? Everyone else had such a huge head start. What if all those years of sitting out in PE made my legs rust?"

"Your legs are not rusty!" Lupe said. "We can totally do this!"

Lupe put the camera down and grabbed the ball out from under me. Then she kicked, and it shot straight past the dumpster, to Billy Bob's room.

"See? It's fun!" she said. "Pretend the laundry room's the goal."

I shook my head.

"Suit yourself," Lupe said, running to get the ball. As she dribbled it toward the laundry room, I stared. I had to admit, it *did* look fun.

She let the ball roll back over to my feet, and I looked down at it again. Then I took a deep breath. *Here goes.* I walked back a few steps, closed my eyes, then ran forward and kicked my "pen." To my surprise, my foot actually hit the ball, and not the parking lot cement block!

I watched as the ball rolled by Lupe to the vending machine. And even though it was nowhere near the laundry room, Lupe threw her hands up and declared, "Goal!"

I laughed.

"Wanna go again?"

I nodded.

Playing with Lupe made my legs loosen up. As we dribbled the ball up and down the lot, Lupe told me that in high school the same thing happened to her sometimes.

"I get so worried thinking about going up against kids who are so much older than me, and I just kind of freeze up."

"Then what do you do?" I asked her.

"I think about how your mom always says, 'Don't worry about what's around you. Or what's behind you. Just focus on what's in front of you.'"

I smiled.

"Thank God she's teaching us," Lupe added. "You should see some of these other schools—they got gifted programs and honors and AP. We don't have any of that."

"Hey!" I reminded her. "Don't worry about what's around you."

Lupe chuckled, and I put her advice into practice. I dribbled the ball to the laundry room and then back to the front office. My feet tripped up a few times, but I just kept trying again.

"That's it! You're getting it!" Lupe yelled excitedly. "Go, Mia!"

I wished my parents could have been there to see it. But the only person who saw us playing was Mr. Yao, who came storming out of the restaurant.

"No soccer in the lot!" he shouted.

"Awww, c'mon!" I crossed my arms, sick of him trying to boss everyone around. "First no math, now no soccer, what next? Is *breathing* only for paying customers too?"

"Do I really need to explain to you this is a business establishment?" he huffed.

"We're still doing business!" I fired back. "I'm totally keeping an eye on the front office. One holler from a guest, and we're there!"

"I don't want you to keep just an eye. I want you to keep a body," he said.

We frowned, but Lupe and I marched back toward the front desk. Then I stopped in my tracks. I had an idea!

"Hey, Mr. Yao, it's gonna be tough for us to rent out more rooms, considering . . ."

"Considering what?" he asked.

"Well, Hank and my dad aren't here, and it's Mrs. Davis's day off.

And all those rooms are dirty," I said, pointing upstairs. "Who's going to clean them?"

It took Mr. Yao a full minute to realize what I was suggesting.

"You want *me* to clean the rooms?"

"It *is* a motel," I reminded him. "And people need rooms."

Lupe muffled a giggle.

"Let's just wait until your dad gets back," he said.

"That could be hours. You know how the lines at the bank are. And do you really want to lose out on all that money we could be making?" I asked.

Mr. Yao shook his head, obviously troubled by this dilemma. "Then *I'll* watch the front desk and you two clean!"

Lupe held up a finger. "It's against the law for children to work with cleaning chemicals."

I grinned. I didn't know if that was a real rule or not, but it sure sounded good!

As Lupe skipped along to the front office, I took Mr. Yao to the laundry room to show him where the cleaning cart and supplies were.

"And this here is the wedge." I held up a block for him. "You put this between the mattress and the box spring, it makes it easier to tuck in—"

"I know what a wedge is!" he snapped. "I was the one who taught you guys, remember?"

I held up my hands. "Okay, okay. Oh, and I almost forgot."

With a smile, I handed him the cleaning uniform my dad and Mrs. Davis wore. It was a blue jumpsuit that said *Cleaning professional in action!*

Mr. Yao shook his head firmly. "I am *not* wearing that thing."

"We're a boutique motel now," I reminded him. "We have to keep our professional image!"

With a sour face, he grabbed the uniform from me and yanked it on.

As Mr. Yao pushed the cart toward room 2, I raced back to the front desk, bursting with giggles. Dad and Hank would be back any second. I had no time to spare!

CHAPTER 21

As Mr. Yao cleaned, Lupe and I ran through the motel, unlocking rooms and messing up beds. We tossed towels on the floor, spilled crackers on the carpet, and put toothpaste on the mirrors. Every time I felt the guilty urge to stop, I thought about my poor parents two years ago, bending over for eighteen hours a day while Mr. Yao barked, "Work harder!"

It was time to give him a taste of his own medicine.

After an hour, he called us at the front desk. "How many more rooms are there?"

"Just a few more!" I chirped.

Lupe nudged me and pointed at the clock. It was nearly 5:00; Mom and Dad would be getting home soon.

"You think one of you girls can come and help me?" Mr. Yao asked, still on the phone. "These sheets are so hard to tuck all by myself!"

"Be right there!"

I found Mr. Yao hunched over the bureau, gasping for breath. He had two big armpit stains on his blue jumper and was fanning himself with a pillowcase. "These ridiculous corners!" He pointed at the fitted sheet. "I can't for the life of me get them to go in! It's like they're trying to kill me!"

"You have the wrong size," I said, showing him the label. He was trying to slap a twin sheet onto a queen bed. "You'd have better luck getting a hot dog into a toothbrush holder."

Mr. Yao kneeled down to look, then collapsed on the floor.

"You know, if you want, I can do the rest," I offered sweetly.

"Thank God," he wheezed, throwing the crumpled sheet in his hand at me.

"But . . . in exchange, you're gonna have to let my mom use her room to teach Lupe and her friends math."

Mr. Yao sat up. He looked around the room, obviously torn between breaking his own no-math rule and resigning himself to more hours of torturous sheet tucking.

"Fine," he hissed through his teeth.

"And let us play soccer!" Lupe added, poking her head in the open door.

"Whatever. Just help me up!"

I reached out a hand to Mr. Yao just as Hank's car pulled in. Right on time! I ran out to wave. My mom was sitting in the passenger side—Hank must have given her a lift home from the high school.

"Hank! Mom! Up here!"

"What's going on?" he called.

Mr. Yao came out in his cleaning jumpsuit. Hank pointed at the feather duster in Mr. Yao's hand as Mom took off her sunglasses.

Hank grinned. "Now *there's* a sight I never thought I'd see!"

CHAPTER 22

Mr. Yao climbed back into his car and left, and Dad finished up cleaning the rest of the rooms. Then, finally, we left to meet our new real estate agent.

"So where is this house?" I asked, running my hands through the air. I was pretending I was petting Comma in the back of the car. I couldn't *wait* to get him, especially now that I knew I could run around and maybe kick a ball to him.

Mia Hamm had been right. Something about playing with your friends, in a relaxed place, took some of the anxiety out of it. I was still not great at it, but at least I didn't turn into stone when the ball touched me.

"It's a sweet little place, over on Chapman, by the river," Mom said. "You're gonna love it!"

"You guys have already seen it? Without me?" I asked, a little hurt. I wanted us to all be together the first time we stepped into our dream house.

But my parents' enthusiasm made me soften.

"It ticks all the boxes. It has a fireplace! And a kitchen island," Dad said, smiling at Mom. "And a perfect little nook for you to write, in the loft upstairs."

"It has a loft?! Can Comma go up there?" I asked. My mind was already teeming with ideas for this nook. I could put a dog bed up there and maybe a little framed corkboard for my story ideas.

"Of course. It's *our* house! We can do whatever we want!" Mom said.

I squealed with excitement as Dad turned onto Chapman.

. . .

Josie, our new agent, was waiting for us at the front door. She was a nice, older white woman with long blond hair that Mom said probably cost a hundred dollars just to wash and blow-dry. It was that shiny.

"You guys are gonna want to make an offer on this place *right away*," Josie said, turning her key in the lock. "We can't wait a second with this one."

She sounded like one of those pushy mall people, trying to get us to buy a heated remote control. But when we stepped inside, I could see why. The place was beautiful!

The walls were freshly painted. There was no hole in the roof! As the fire crackled from the fireplace, Mom spun around the living room.

I raced up the stairs two at a time and found the loft, next to the bedrooms. It was just like my parents said—perfect for writing! It even had a beautiful wooden desk built into the wall. I took my place in the chair.

"This is amazing!" I called out to Mom. The desk was big enough to hold all my binders with my columns, and I still would have room to put up a corkboard.

I ran to the stair railing and looked down at my parents. Mom and Dad were dancing in the living room—they looked so happy. I smiled. I bet Dad missed Mom while she slept in the guest room all these months.

"And look, there's finally enough space for a real Christmas tree," Dad said, pointing to the bright area right beside the fireplace, bathed with sunlight.

Though we always got a small plastic tree to put on the front desk, we'd never had a *real* tree before. My eyes lit up.

"And a small orange tree at Lunar New Year!" Mom added.

I walked back downstairs to join my parents in the living room. I imagined Comma running back and forth from the Christmas tree and the orange tree. Lunar New Year was usually a month or two after Christmas. Still, I decided that in our family, we'd leave them both up until at least March.

Mom walked into the kitchen and leaned against the beautiful kitchen island. "What's the next step? We put in an offer?" she asked.

"Yes," Josie said. "I can start the paperwork."

Mom looked to Dad. "Can we really afford this?"

Josie cut in. "It's an older unit, built in the sixties. So it's not as pricey. But it'll go quick. We have to move on it!"

Eagerly, my parents nodded. It was decided. We were making an offer!

I put my hand over my thundering heart. I could hardly keep it from leaping out. *We're doing this! We're buying our first American house!*

• • •

I could hardly sleep a wink that night. I wanted to start moving my stuff already!

About the tenth time I woke up, I slipped out of bed and went to get some water. Through the window, I spotted Hank out by the vending machines. I snuck out back to talk to him.

"What are you doing up so late?" he asked.

"I couldn't sleep. I'm too excited about the house!"

Hank laughed as he reached for his soda. "I remember that feeling! There's nothing quite like it."

Hank got an extra soda out and handed it to me. I opened my can, and we bumped our two cream sodas together.

"How'd it go with the lawyers today?" I asked as I took a sip.

"Well, the good news is, it's not completely like what Wamble said. I may have some sort of claim under trade secrets."

"That's great! It was totally a secret! That's why it's called your *secret* recipe!" I said.

"We'd have to prove it, and that might take months."

"But there's a chance, right?" I asked. With a grin, I added, "Where there's a will, there's a way!"

Hank tapped on his soda can. "An *expensive* way."

In the moonlight, I asked quietly, "How expensive?"

"Going up against a big competitor like the Grill?" Hank whistled. "It'll take hundreds of hours of lawyer time, at three hundred dollars an hour."

I nearly dropped my can.

"I'd probably have to sell my condo."

"*What??*" I shook my head vigorously. "No way." Now that I knew how hard it was to buy a house, I couldn't let Hank give up his condo. "What about Ms. Patel, the pro bono lawyer?" I asked.

"I called her; she only does immigration cases for free. She actually urged me to drop it. . . . Said the big guys usually win. Even if I manage to convince the judge, the process will bleed me dry."

My fingers turned as ice cold as the sodas. We should have never gone into the Grill.

"There has to be another way," I said. "What about if I write an article? Expose them?"

Hank shook his head. It was the first time his eyes did not light up at the idea of me writing something. "If you write about it, they could sue me for defamation. Claim I'm making it up."

"Not if it's true!"

"We'd have to prove that in court," he said. "And again, that's expensive."

I kicked the vending machine. It was *so unfair*. "So what are you going to do?"

"I could just let it go, but I keep thinking, what about the next guy? And the person after that? What if he's in an even weaker position than me? They'll never stop unless *somebody* stands up to them!"

I understood then that it was a matter of principle for Hank. Win or lose, he wanted to tell them it was *not okay* to steal from the little guy. That was what he'd be selling his condo for.

Hank sank his face into his hands. "I just want to compete, fair and square. Earn my slice of the American dream, without worrying the pieces I've built are gonna get pinched."

I wanted that so desperately for him too. For all of us.

"I know it's just a recipe . . . but it's *my* recipe."

"Oh, Hank." I hugged him tight. It wasn't just a recipe, it was what the recipe symbolized: the fact that anyone anywhere in America could come up with a good idea and make it. That was what the Grill had stolen.

I put my hand on Hank's shoulder, wishing I knew what to do. But for once, I didn't have the words.

CHAPTER 23

Da-Shawn caught up with me, carrying a folder of papers, as I was coming out of the library on my way to PE the next day. I had been researching, and Hank was right—it was going to be hard to prove that the recipe was indeed a trade secret.

I told Da-Shawn about it as we walked.

"Are you sure we can't just write an article and expose them?" I asked Da-Shawn.

"A big restaurant like the Grill? It's too risky. It'll be their word against ours, and if they come after us, we could get in trouble with the school. Maybe even lose our News Room."

I sighed. I could already hear Bethany's off-tune gloating in my head.

Da-Shawn put a finger to his chin. "But maybe we can run a student review of their new burger."

"A review? That'll just give them more publicity!" I protested. "*Unless* . . . you mean we give them a really *bad* review," I said, a wicked smile forming. But Da-Shawn shook his head.

"Sorry, Mia, you can't be the one to write it."

I crossed my arms. "Why not?"

"Because it's a conflict of interest. Since you're an owner of the Calivista restaurant, you can't give an unbiased opinion of the Grill. They're your competition."

"Can too!" I protested.

Da-Shawn gave me a look, and I hushed up. *Okay, maybe I can't.*

"It wouldn't be fair, just like it wouldn't be fair not to include Bethany's 'Dear Future Me' letter," Da-Shawn reminded me.

"Which was totally phony, by the way."

"Totally."

"So what do we do?" I asked.

"We can try contacting a reporter at a bigger paper," he suggested. "See if they can help?"

I shook my head. I was used to picking up my pen and solving my own problems, not finding someone "bigger."

"Chop-chop, Mia!" Mr. Antwell called. "Stop dawdling!"

"I'm not dawdling," I called back. "We're discussing how to take down a major Los Angeles restaurant!"

"Exactly," Da-Shawn said as he handed me that week's student submissions to copyedit. "The Grill is an institution! We can't just take them down with a student article. That'll be like going to war with a water gun! We need a *cannon*!"

As I stuffed the papers into my backpack and hustled over to the field, I pictured the soccer balls on the field as cannons. I frowned, sick and tired of having the Grill win just by virtue of their size, before anyone had even heard our side of the argument. When Mr. Antwell blew on his whistle, I threw down my backpack and kicked the soccer ball with all my rage.

"That's it, Mia! Now you're getting it!" Mr. Antwell said. "Keep going!"

I turned to him, surprised.

Jason grinned at me and kicked the ball back. "Do it again!" he encouraged.

I closed my eyes and pictured Mr. Wamble's head on the ball. When I looked up, the ball was all the way on the other side of the field. Maybe the key to doing sports was tricking yourself into thinking you're kicking a hamburger crook!

"Mia! Shoot it!" my teammates cried.

I pointed to my chest. *Who, me?* But my legs were already moving, running across the field to try for a goal. Unfortunately, just as I was about to kick the ball again, I slipped on a wet patch of grass and fell. Bethany dived in and stole my ball, shooting it in the opposite direction.

I jumped back to my feet and threw my arms in the air. I hadn't scored, but I also wasn't scared anymore. Bethany's long legs came right at me, and I ran right back at her!

Even Mr. Antwell was impressed. "That was great, Mia," he said after the game. "You got in there! You didn't chicken out!"

"Thanks, Mr. A!"

Jason ran up and gave me a high five. "You were on fire!" he said. "We still on for after school? My garage?"

"Absolutely!"

As Jason and I walked back from PE and he updated me on the leak progress at his house, Bethany strutted by us, rolling her eyes.

"MOVE," she harrumphed.

"We are," Jason said.

Bethany turned around. She looked at me and added, "You're still the slowest person out there."

My face turned beet red.

"Whoa!" Jason protested. "That was totally uncalled—"

I shook my head and walked up to Bethany. "Maybe. But you know what? I'm just getting started. I have a *long* way to go. And if you're nervous now, just wait . . ."

With that, I strolled calmly toward the changing rooms, slowly but surely, while Bethany stared. Nothing scares people more than fear.

I should know.

• • •

The leak in the Yaos' garage was next to the water heater, and Mrs. Yao managed to section it off and put a giant bucket there. Still, the boxes that Jason and I wanted to look through were all soaking wet on the bottom. Maybe Mr. Yao was right that home ownership wasn't all that it was cracked up to be.

Jason set the boxes down on a fluffy towel, and we started digging.

"Dad says there's no recipes or anything in there. And he wants all this stuff gone by the end of the week," Jason said. "But I already found a couple."

"A couple more diary entries?" I asked, perking up.

Jason shook his head. "No. Recipes from my grandparents. I have them in my room! Be right back!"

I found old ledgers and receipts and even unused napkins—leave it to Mr. Yao to save everything! I picked up the napkins delicately, trying to save them from the musty wet box. They read *Yao's Kitchen*. I held one up to my nose, trying to see if I could smell highlighter chicken on it. But it had been too many years.

Then my eye caught the shiny gleam of metal. A spiral notebook! I dug it out. On the cover were the words *DO NOT READ*.

"Jackpot!" I shouted.

I looked around for Jason, but he was still up in his room. I couldn't wait. I turned to the first page and started reading.

Dear diary,
Dad's back is a little better, so he's at the wok again. Thank God, because my highlighter chicken was turning into eraser chicken.

Today a really embarrassing thing happened. One of my classmates, Jimmy Vanderbean, came in with his family. Jimmy Vanderbean, if you remember, is the guy who called me "Brass Gas" in band. (For the record, I farted ONCE while playing my trumpet.) But the Brass Gas name stuck, and he walks around saying I should just quit—whoever heard of a good Chinese trumpet player anyway?

So Jimmy came in on Sunday with his family. I hid underneath a table, but my mom yelled, "Michael!!! Get them some tea!!!"

She's always on my case about bringing out the tea before the customer can say "Just some ice water, please." We can charge for tea, but not for water. So there I was, pouring tea for Jimmy and his twin sisters, trying hard to avoid his gaze, when Jimmy registers me. He spills his tea ALL OVER THE TABLE.

He starts dabbing up the mess with napkins, but his mom yells at him to stop.

"Jimmy. Let them do it! That's what we pay 'em for!"

Can you believe that? That's what she said to him! So I kneeled and started wiping, because of course Jimmy had to spill it all over the floor. And I'm two inches from his feet, smelling his horrendous socks.

That's when Jimmy's mom shrieks, "Hey, aren't you in Jimmy's class?"

At first, I tried to pretend I don't speak English. But then she said, "Yeah! You're the boy in his marching band. With the crooked plume!"

For the record, yes, I have a crooked plume. That's because Dad refused to get the box for it. It cost five whole extra dollars!

Anyway, my cheeks grew hotter than Dad's wok. I stayed wiping the floor underneath Jimmy's table long after the tea dried up.

In the end, they didn't even leave a tip. And GET THIS. At school on Monday, he lied and told everyone he went to Denny's after church for lunch, not to our restaurant! Which I suppose is a good thing. But still. It hurt because the food we make is so good.

Hopefully one day I'll look back, when I'm traveling through Europe as a world-renowned trumpet player, and this will all seem funny. Until then, it sure sucks lychees.

Michael Yao

I jumped when Jason came back in and announced, "Here are the recipes!"

"Jason! Come look at this!" I cried. "You didn't tell me your dad plays the trumpet!"

"He *does*??" Jason asked, running over.

I showed him the diary entry.

"That's so weird! He's never played for us before!" Jason walked around the garage, moving old rugs and looking under moldy hats. "And I don't see one here anywhere!"

"Maybe he quit?" I asked, feeling a pang of sadness. I wished young Michael had gone on his European tour, but I was pretty sure that never happened.

Jason flipped frantically to a new page in the notebook, but there were no more entries. He sat down on the cold garage floor and looked over his father's words once again. "Man, the way he describes that shame . . . not wanting to have your classmates find out. That's how I felt too."

"What do you mean, you felt it too?" I asked, surprised. "You guys *owned* the Calivista!"

"So? It was still just a motel."

"*Just* a motel?" If my family had owned thirty-plus rooms *and* a pool, two vending machines, and don't even get me started on

ALL the TVs, I would have been as proud as the sun. I *was* as proud as the sun!

"It's not exactly something you heard other kids talking about," Jason confessed. "Until you came along." He looked up at me and smiled. "You made it *cool* to work in a motel," he said shyly.

I smiled back and bumped my shoulder lightly against his. "It *is* cool. And so is working in a restaurant."

Jason nodded wholeheartedly.

I jumped up and opened a couple more boxes. "Where did you say your grandparents' restaurant was?"

"In the San Gabriel Valley somewhere." He set the journal down and helped me.

We dug through the boxes until Jason found a card for Yao's Kitchen with an address—it was on Elm Street in Pasadena!

"I thought I'd called every single Chinese restaurant in Pasadena, but I don't remember calling any on Elm Street! You think it's still there?"

"We should go check it out!" Jason said excitedly.

We looked around for a map and finally found a dusty old Thomas Guide next to Mr. Yao's old bowling ball. We'd just opened it when Mr. Yao himself walked in.

"What are you guys doing?" he asked. "You shouldn't be playing around here. You're gonna make the leak worse!"

"We're not even touching the leak," Jason argued. "Just sorting through the boxes."

"I thought I said I wanted all that stuff gone!"

"We have to go through it first!" Jason snapped.

Mr. Yao started grabbing the boxes away from us. I quickly tucked his journal behind my jacket.

"You're not going through anything! You should be at the restaurant!" Mr. Yao barked. "You made me sink eight hundred dollars into the restaurant, and now all the flowers are rotting! And the soccer players—where are they?"

Jason flushed. "I don't know, Dad. Maybe they're—"

"They're not coming!" Mr. Yao pointed to Jason. "And I'll tell you why. You should have never said to them we make Chinese food—this is all your fault!"

The difference between the nice, sensitive boy in the diaries and the angry, screaming man in front of us was jarring.

"No it's *not*!" I said. Jason cowered next to me, the same way I did in PE class. I threw his own line from his diary back at Mr. Yao. "When you say it like that, it hurts, because the food we make is so good!"

But Mr. Yao didn't remember his childhood words. "It's good to *us*," he said. "But to white people, it's just fast food. Not a *real* restaurant."

Jason clenched his jaw, clearly stung. But he remained silent, his eyes glued to the floor.

"Then why'd you invest in it?" I asked.

"Yeah." Jason looked up. "Why did you invest in *my* restaurant?"

"I wanted to set you up. Help you succeed. But you have to listen to me—"

"*That's* why?" Jason cut him off. His eyes filled with hurt. "You wanted to buy my success?"

Mr. Yao hesitated. "I just don't want to see you suffer."

"You won't have to, because I quit," Jason said. Then he grabbed his jacket and ran out of the garage.

CHAPTER 24

I chased Jason all the way to the end of his cul-de-sac. He was hiding behind a tree by the side of a small, narrow creek.

"I hate him!" Jason said when I took my shoes off and sat down nearby. "I never want to talk to him again."

I peered at my friend. I knew how hurt he was; it was the same way I felt all those years ago, but it must ache so much more because it was his *dad*.

"I'm sorry he said that," I said. "He doesn't mean it."

"Oh, he meant it all right. Just like he meant it when he called me fat growing up. Or the time he made fun of my math, remember that?"

I nodded weakly.

"Or called my handwriting chicken poop!"

Jason continued listing one thing after another. Gently, I put a hand on his arm. "Your dad is just . . . your dad. But you can't quit on your dreams because of what he says. He's one person."

"But he means *everything*." Jason rubbed his eyes.

I hated seeing Jason like this.

He blew his nose into his arm and cried, "All I wanted was for him to see me in my element and be proud of me. I was so excited when he said he wanted to invest. Now I just walk around with a giant knot in my stomach, worrying what new criticism is gonna come flying out of his mouth."

An angry, booming voice called out from the street, "Jason?" It was Mr. Yao coming out to look for him. Jason got an armful of leaves and covered both of us. We sat quiet as bedbugs as Mr. Yao stomped up and down the cul-de-sac, yelling. Finally, when he gave up and went home, Jason and I reemerged from the leaves.

"We'll tell him to back off," I said. "I'll help you."

"He'll never change. It's too much."

"Hey, if I can get through it with him, so can you!"

Jason took a rock and threw it into the stream. "Yeah, well, you didn't have to live with him."

• • •

When my dad picked me up, Jason came with us to get his things from the Calivista.

"You're not really *quitting* quitting, are you?" I asked him in the car.

"I don't know," he said.

"Please don't," I begged. "We need you."

"Jason, I know you're going through a lot," Dad said from the front. "But think of all your customers . . ."

"They'll survive," Jason muttered.

I turned to him with moist eyes—how could he say that?—but the sad look on his face broke my heart. He would miss his customers more than anyone, I could tell.

I reached for his hand, but he pulled away.

"No," he snapped. "I'm fine."

I swallowed hard and stared straight ahead. As soon as my dad pulled into our parking lot, I bolted out the door to find Hank. He was in the kitchen chopping carrots. Jason walked in behind me before I could say anything, though, and started packing up his cutting knives and mixing spoons.

"Hey, bud," Hank said to Jason. "Where you taking all that? The dinner rush's about to start."

Jason glanced toward the dining room, torn.

"I'm so sorry. I can't stay today," Jason finally said. "I got some stuff on my mind."

"What's wrong?" Hank asked.

Jason shook his head.

"Out with it, and we can chop it up. That's what we always do," Hank encouraged him, taking Jason's apron off the hanger and handing it to him. "Pour all your frustrations into the stew, and watch the steam carry your anger away."

Jason shook his head again. "Not this time—this is one pickle we can't chop up."

"Even the sourest of sauerkraut doesn't taste so sour if you get it off your chest," Hank said, holding out a fermented cabbage leaf from one of Jason's kimchi jars.

Jason loved kimchi. He looked at it for a long while. Then he put it in his mouth and reached for his apron.

"I'll stay, but only if you tell my dad I'm not here," he said.

"We won't breathe a word," Hank promised.

"What if he comes in here looking for you?" I asked.

Jason bit his lower lip, then pointed toward the manager's quarters. "I'll cook from your kitchen, Mia," he said. "He'll never look in there."

Hank chuckled. "Hey, works for me! I don't care where you're cooking, as long as you're doing what you love." He gave Jason a hug and sent him to the manager's quarters, along with a big basket of cabbage.

CHAPTER 25

For the next two days, Jason cooked out of our tiny kitchen in the manager's quarters while I carried the food back and forth. When Mr. Yao came around, Jason slipped out the back and joined Lupe and her Math Cup friends in Mom's room. They were prepping for their big competition on Monday.

Mr. Yao found me in the restaurant on Friday. "Where in the world is Jason?" he demanded, picking up a spring roll with his fingers. "He disappears after school and doesn't come home until late. He says he's at the library, but he's not!"

"I don't know where he is," I said, waving him away from the food. "I only know you need to apologize to him."

"I'm not apologizing." Mr. Yao frowned, pointing to the shrimp dumplings in the bamboo steam tray. "And where are you guys getting all these dumplings?"

"We . . . er . . . had a lot left over in the freezer." I followed him out to the cashier's desk in the dining room.

"That's a relief. I thought I would have to buy trays of wontons from the other Asian place in town and sell them as ours!"

"Can't you see this is hurting the restaurant?" I asked. I was tired of running food back and forth. Either Mr. Yao apologized, or I would have to invest in a pair of Rollerblades!

"Talk to him and make things right! *Please*."

Mr. Yao banged open the cash tray. "If he doesn't want to be here because he has a problem with authority, then he shouldn't—"

"He doesn't have a problem with authority!" I cried. "He has a problem with *you*. You're way too harsh, and you don't ever listen to him!"

"Because he's a kid!"

"So?"

There was a loud *CLANG* from Mr. Yao slamming the cash tray.

"So that's how it works," he barked. "And if he doesn't like it, he can sleep in the library." As usual, Mr. Yao's pride got the better of him. As he walked out in a huff, I shook my head, taking the shrimp dumplings off the steamer. They were soggy now, and I didn't know how to fix them. I gazed in the direction of Mom's guest room as Hank walked back in.

"How'd it go?" I asked him. He'd gone to meet with his lawyers to talk about the Grill.

"Good! My team thinks I got a chance. We'll see. We're meeting with the Grill lawyers next week. Gonna give them one last chance to make things right."

I threw out the soggy dumplings and washed out the bamboo steamer. "What are you going to ask for?"

"I want an apology, profit sharing on the burgers, and, most of all, formal recognition that it's my creation," he said, ticking each item off on his fingers.

"That sounds more than fair!" I said.

"Let's hope they agree, because I can't afford to go to court. . . ." His voice trailed off, and he looked down at his hands. "I took out a new loan on my condo, just to afford my lawyer's fees."

My chest squeezed as tight as a spring roll when I heard that. I thought about how much the condo meant to Hank and the *years* of blood, sweat, and tears it took to get it. "What did it cost?" I asked. "We could have helped!"

"You guys are trying to buy your own home. This is my battle to fight."

I sighed. It hardly seemed fair that he'd have to put his hard-earned home on the line, just to make things right.

"Jason still avoiding his dad?" Hank asked.

I nodded. "He's back there with my mom, hiding."

"Poor kid. I have an idea. Let's take him out tomorrow to cheer him up!"

My eyes brightened. "Maybe we can go to his grandparents' restaurant on Elm Street tomorrow—if it's still around. It's in Pasadena!"

"Great idea!" Hank walked over to the sink and held up one of the soggy dumplings. He smiled as he hollered, "Hey, this looks like an eraser. Tell me you haven't been writing at the stove."

I chuckled, but then I remembered what Mr. Yao said about eraser chicken in his diary. I felt regret settle in my tummy. I wished I'd gotten through to Mr. Yao. Maybe if I'd asked him how he'd feel if he were in Jason's shoes, being told what to do by *his* dad all the time, not getting a chance to prove himself on his own—just maybe I could have pierced through his stubbornness and anger. But I didn't have the courage. Not yet.

CHAPTER 26

Bright and early on Saturday, Hank, Lupe, and I went to pick up Jason. There were workers all over the place to fix the garage leak. Mr. Yao wanted Jason to stay and watch, but his mother wanted to get him out of the house.

"You don't know how hard it is to schedule these guys," Mrs. Yao said to us as she ran around her garage, directing the workers. "Your parents are so lucky you're not homeowners!"

"Actually, my dad's working on changing that!" I beamed proudly. Josie, our agent, had submitted our offer.

Hank turned to Mr. Yao. "Why didn't you tell us you had a leak? I could have taken a look at it for you."

"We're *fine*, thank you," Mr. Yao snapped.

Hank took a step back, his eyebrows up in an *all righty, then* expression.

Jason climbed into the car, slamming the door hard behind him. I rolled down my window and called out to Mr. Yao, "We're going to Pasadena. Elm Street!"

I wanted to see his reaction. But he kept his gaze steady on the garage, so I rolled my window back up. Lupe caught my eye and shrugged.

"Thanks for doing this, Hank!" Jason said, grinning and giving

Hank an air high five as we pulled out of the driveway.

Hank air-high-fived him back. "Are you kidding? This is your family's culinary history we're talking about! I know how much that means to you."

"I hope it's still in business," I said.

"Me too! I'm starving! I've been too nervous to eat my dinner the last few nights!" Lupe said. "Our first ever intra-district math competition's on Monday!"

"You guys ready?" I asked.

Lupe hesitated for a second before nodding. "Think so. Allie and I were on the phone practicing last night until ten."

"How's she doing?" I asked. I'd caught a glimpse of Allie in Mom's room the other day with the rest of the team. She had long red hair and glasses, and she was asking my mom questions. She seemed very polite.

"Super smart. And totally down to earth. She loves hiking and swimming! Oh, and she doesn't want to shave her legs either when she grows up!"

Jason made a face. "So she's going to have big old hairy legs like a caterpillar?!"

"Who are you calling a caterpillar?" Lupe rolled up her sleeves like she was getting ready to fight.

I giggled, and Hank raised an eyebrow in the rearview mirror.

"If we're caterpillars, you guys are sea otters!" Lupe continued.

"So?" Jason asked, peering down at the hairs on his arms.

"So why should we shave our legs, if you sea otters are just going to lounge around, being all furry?"

"I didn't make the rules!" Jason protested.

"Well, they're not good rules," Lupe said. "And me and Allie intend to change them."

"Me too!" I added.

Lupe smiled.

"So tell us more about this Allie," Jason asked, still peering at his own arm hair. "Is she good at anything else, besides math?"

"Yeah! She told me she makes a really good avocado summer roll."

"Ooh! Avocado summer rolls—we should try that!" Jason said, sitting up straighter. "We could wrap it in a thin rice paper wrapper!"

"We could have a taste test! See which one's better!" Lupe said. "That would be super fun!"

"Another reason for you to come back to the *real* kitchen." I nudged Jason.

He looked down. "Yeah. But I really can't work with my dad anymore. He didn't even apologize."

"I know how you feel," Hank called out from the front. "Believe me, I do. I'm still fighting with the Grill just to get an apology. And they may or they may not. But I'm not gonna let it stop me from doing what I love, which is cooking up good food that people enjoy."

Jason nodded slowly.

"Your customers are all asking about you," I added, putting a hand on his shoulder. "Don't you miss seeing their faces?"

Jason glanced down at his grandparents' business card in his hand. "Course I miss it. I wish we could put in a camera so I can see them!" Jason sighed. "But I *don't* miss the pit in my stomach from being judged all day long by my dad."

"I hear ya," Hank said, glancing in the mirror as we got off in Pasadena.

I wished Mr. Yao could have been there to hear Jason pour his heart out. Then again, there was no telling what he might have said. Maybe it was better for Jason to cook in the manager's quarters for now and not find out.

Then Hank turned us onto Elm Street, and Jason pointed.

"There it is!!!" he shouted.

We pressed our noses against the window, staring at the small Chinese restaurant on the corner of Elm and Hill Street called Lotus Garden. It had jade-green walls and a bright red door. There was a Chinese sign on the window that said *OPEN*.

Jason bounced in his seat, while I snapped a photo with my Polaroid. I'd never see him so excited before, not even the time when miso was on sale at the store for $1.50! Lupe giggled. Hank dropped us off, telling us he'd be back in an hour. He was going to the Pasadena library to look up more information on trade secrets.

"Take all the time in the world!" Jason hollered as he ran toward the restaurant.

CHAPTER 27

Pushing the doors of Lotus Garden open, I felt like we were stepping into a time capsule. The lights hung down in red lanterns from the ceiling. There was an enormous Chinese watercolor painting on one wall. But the thing that really caught my eye was a neon sign that said, *An American Chinese Restaurant*.

I snapped a photo of the sign for my cousin Shen. He'd get a kick out of it, and then he'd probably debate me for an hour, that it wasn't possible for a restaurant to be *both* American and Chinese.

Jason noticed it too. "Look at that!" he said. "You think my folks put that there?"

He skipped over to touch it as I stared at the words. Young Michael Yao definitely believed a restaurant could be both, but old cranky Mr. Yao now insisted a Chinese restaurant was *just* a Chinese restaurant. I wondered when he'd changed his opinion.

"Excuse me, may we speak to the owner?" I asked one of the waitresses.

She nodded, but before she could move, a little boy, about four years old, walked out from the kitchen and headed straight for her. I smiled at him and exchanged a look with Lupe. He was just like us but younger. He hugged the waitress's leg, and I figured he must be her son. I kneeled down and held my hand out for him to high-five.

An older couple walked over. "We're the owners," the woman said. "Can I help you?"

Jason immediately stuck out his hand. "Hi, I'm Jason Yao, and these are my friends Mia and Lupe. This used to be my grandparents' restaurant!"

The elderly couple's eyes smiled at him as they shook his hand. "Welcome!" the man said. "We're Mr. and Mrs. Wong. I never met your grandparents, but I met your father."

"Wow, really??" Jason cried.

The Wongs nodded. "He's the one who sold us the restaurant, right after your grandparents passed," said Mrs. Wong. "How's he doing?"

"Good!" Jason said.

"He still in the restaurant business?"

"Sorta," Jason said.

Mr. Wong chuckled. "I always knew he had a very lucky face."

They led us into the kitchen and pointed to a small wooden table in the back, next to the supplies closet. The table had a little stool, and it was covered with pencil markings. "Your father told me this used to be where he did his homework as a kid."

Jason kneeled down and ran his fingers across the scratched wooden surface.

"Mia! Look at this!" He pointed to the letters *M.Y.* etched onto the table. I got down too, and a thrill tingled through me as I felt Mr. Yao's initials. It was so weird—one minute we were reading his letters, and now here we were *with him*!

"We kept it all these years," Mrs. Wong said. "It was where our daughter did her homework, and our grandson will too." They nodded at the little boy toddling into the kitchen.

"Can we stay here for a minute?" Jason asked.

"Sure!" Mr. Wong said. "Stay as long as you want. We're just preparing some to-go orders."

The couple left us, and Jason, Lupe, and I sat on the floor. Jason hugged one leg of the table, as though just touching it brought him closer to his dad.

"You think this is where he wrote all those diaries?" I asked, handing Lupe the latest one we'd found.

"He sounds *so* different," Lupe said, her eyes scanning the page.

"I wish I could go back in time and be his friend. Maybe then he'd say something nice to me," Jason said, sticking his head underneath the table. "Hey! There's a message here."

Lupe and I both ducked under at the same time, colliding.

"Oww," I said, rubbing my head. "What's it say?"

"'Flour sack,'" Jason said. He furrowed his eyebrows as we all sat back up. *"Flour sack?"*

"Maybe he liked messing around with play dough?" I guessed.

We turned to Mr. and Mrs. Wong, busy rolling out noodles by hand in the kitchen. There was a huge sack of flour next to them. "Excuse me, can I see where you keep the rest of your flour?" I asked the Wongs, getting up.

They pointed to an open cabinet.

"Here!" Mrs. Wong said. "This cabinet is deep enough to hold all the flour, and we need *lots*, don't we?"

"And I play hide-and-seek in there!" the little boy piped up, crawling inside to demonstrate.

"You wouldn't believe how many dumplings people order," Mr. Wong said.

"But you're not in the yellow pages!" I said.

"It's all word of mouth!" Mrs. Wong told me. "Years of making the thinnest *pier* by hand, and the thickest dumpling *tang*."

We peered inside the cabinet as Mr. and Mrs. Wong helped us move the flour sacks out. It sure was deep, almost as big as the walk-in closet at the Chapman Street house we were buying. At the thought of the house, my lungs squeezed so tight I could hardly breathe. I wondered if the sellers had reviewed our offer by now. I crossed all my fingers and toes, hoping they'd take it!

As Jason got the sacks out, Lupe and I opened up every one, hoping we'd find a jackpot of old letters, but there was nothing but flour. When we got to the last one, our shoulders sank.

"Nothing in this one either," Lupe sighed.

Jason crawled out of the cabinet. Seeing the look on his face, I went back to the table and stared underneath it one more time. Next to the words *FLOUR SACK*, I noticed a small carved rectangle.

"Maybe it's not the sack!" I cried, rushing back to the cabinet. This time, when I got all the way in the very back, I pushed on the wall. To my surprise, the thin piece of wood fell right onto my lap. It was movable! Carefully, I crawled back out with it. There, taped on the other side, was an envelope.

"I found something!"

CHAPTER 28

The edges of the taped brown manila envelope were tattered and wrinkled. It had obviously been there for decades. Without wasting another minute, Jason poured its contents out. Pages and pages of handwritten notes from Michael Yao spilled onto the table, along with magazine articles and sheet music.

We whooped with excitement.

"This must have been his secret hiding place!" Jason cried.

I took one of the handwritten notes and read it aloud.

Dear diary,

I keep telling Dad to go to the doctor—he fell at the wok yesterday—but as usual, he refuses. Dad has a deep suspicion of doctors in the US. He thinks they're all out to scam him. They'll make him do expensive tests and painful procedures even when he's running okay. And he'll come out like a lobotomized scarecrow, with his big toe on top of his head.

I tried to tell him that's not going to happen. But he won't listen. A few times, I caught him at the stove, wheezing a little.

like he was trying to catch his breath.

But he just drinks his cupful of oolong tea and tells me, "Bei guan wo, zuo ni di shi." Don't care about me, do your work.

How do I tell him I do care about him? White people, they're always saying they love each other. Like every two seconds on TV. "Love you!" "Love you too!"

It's gotta be massively embarrassing, confessing your love all the time. But sometimes I wish we had a system like that too. Instead, we just shove food at each other. And I don't know how to get Dad to a doctor, short of telling him there's a shiitake mushroom sale at the doctor's office.

Sometimes I wish my parents were like everyone else's.

Michael Yao

I chuckled at the shiitake mushroom bit. Michael was pretty funny. And I knew exactly how he felt. My parents were the same way. For years, they were scared to go to the doctor. Whenever I got sick, Mom would pull out the big gingery-smelling suitcase under her bed—the one that was filled with Chinese medicine—and brew me some soup that for all I knew was made out of light bulbs.

Another reason I was so deathly afraid of the soccer ball for so long.

"Listen to this one!" Lupe said, and started reading to us.

Dear diary,
Dad finally agreed to go see the doctor.

Mom asked me to make an appointment for him. So I got on the phone. I'm always the one making the call whenever there's anything official. One time the telephone company overcharged my mom, I had to pretend I was her. Now that my voice is changing, it's NOT that easy.

Anyway, I sat on hold for forty-five minutes trying to make Dad an appointment. When I got through, they asked me for my name. I told them Dad's name. I thought it would be quick and simple, but the guy spent five whole minutes making me repeat it. "Bu Fu Yao? You joking, right? Bu Fu?? That's your name??!"

I wanted to throw the phone across the room. No wonder Dad doesn't like doctors. I don't blame him after that. Anyway, the appointment is on Tuesday. I'm gonna go with him, and if they try any of that BU FU WHAT? stuff again, I'm going to give them a boo-hoo they'll remember.

Michael Yao

"That's so mean," Lupe said, shaking her head when she finished reading. "Poor Michael. I have to do that too, get on the phone with the credit card company and the bank, pretending to be my mom."

"Here's another one," Jason said, joining the read-aloud.

Dear diary,
The appointment went well. Doc says the wheezing was from stress. Dad just needs to rest. The doctor was very nice. No one said anything about his name.

When we got back, there were seven tables waiting. Mom was trying her best to keep up with the orders by herself, but the customers kept complaining service was too slow. One guy got so mad, he called Dad a name. A name I am NEVER going to repeat. I have been called this at school a few times before, but it made my blood boil hearing someone call my dad that. I told him to shut up, and we got into a fight. Dad ran out and stopped us. Then he made ME apologize.

Afterward, he said I can't fight with a customer EVER. Because the customer is always right.

I can't describe the feeling of being attacked and then told by my own dad that we have to apologize. That we have to live with it. That this is the price of doing business.

I wish I hadn't taken him to the doctor's appointment.

Michael Yao

I looked at Jason, my eyes wet. He was hugging the letter to his chest. I just wanted to jump into the paper and tell young Michael, *You don't. You don't have to live with it!*

"Now it makes sense why he's so angry," Lupe said. "He had to deal with so much trauma. He didn't even have parents who . . ."

Her voice hitched as she looked at Jason.

"You can say it," Jason muttered. "He didn't even have parents who supported him."

Slowly, Jason stuffed the rest of the letters in the envelope and handed them to me. Then he stood up.

"Don't you want to keep reading?" I asked.

But he just walked out of the kitchen.

I followed him, thanking the Wongs and giving them my card. "By the way, if anyone calls from a hotel for a large order of dumplings, give me a call? We're trying to find the Chinese women's soccer team."

Mr. and Mrs. Wong promised they would.

Out in the parking lot, I found Jason sitting on a rock, waiting for Hank to pick us up. I tried giving him back the envelope, but he shook his head.

"The more I read, the more I think I'm gonna turn out just like him."

"What?" I said. "That's ridiculous."

"His parents didn't care about how he was feeling. They yelled at him when all he was trying to do was stand up for them!" Jason's tears fell onto the hot cement at our feet. "Don't you see how alike we are?"

It pained me so much to see my friend hurting this way. "That's not going to happen to you," I insisted.

"Why not?"

Lupe walked over. We looked at each other and then at Jason.

"Because you have us," I said. "And you have Michael Yao. He's *in* there." I pointed to the letters. "And he's in your dad too. You gotta believe that. If you don't give up on him, he's not going to give up on you."

CHAPTER 29

Later that day, after we dropped Jason off at home and Lupe was at Math Cup practice in Mom's room, I sat at the front desk with Michael Yao's diary entries. There were at least a half dozen more about his dad's health, as well as a few really funny ones on his many marching band field trips. I couldn't stop reading.

Dear diary,
Today in band, Mr. B asked me to lead the class. He had a bad sore throat from eating too many hot chili peppers. I knew nothing about conducting. But it was really fun. It was nice being the leader of the band—the big CHEESE, as Mr. B calls it.

I liked how everyone came together as a team. I complimented the brass section, even though I could totally hear Jimmy playing a wrong note. But I figure everyone could use a compliment!

Mr. B said I did a good job. I know I told my parents I only took marching band to get out of PE, but I could see myself leading a band one day, maybe even touring all over the world. I would love to go somewhere—ANYWHERE other than sitting in the kitchen, sweating it out.

Michael Yao

My mind exploded with questions. Mr. Yao wanted to be a band leader?? He took marching band to get out of PE?? I didn't even know you can do that! And he actually complimented people?!

I hopped off the stool and walked over to the photocopy machine to make a duplicate of that line because it was so mind-blowing.

Dad walked in then and asked, "Did Josie the agent call?"

I shook my head. "Nope."

He leaned over to read my enlarged copy of *Everyone could use a compliment!* "Where's that from?"

"Mr. Yao!"

He jumped. "*Our* Mr. Yao?"

"He was a completely different guy when he was younger." I scooted over so Dad could see Mr. Yao's diary entries for himself. As he read, the phone rang.

I picked it up, hoping it was Mr. and Mrs. Wong calling from the restaurant with a lead for Team China. "Calivista Motel, this is Mia!"

"Hi, Mia. It's Josie, your realtor. Are your parents there?"

"Yes!" I exclaimed, handing the phone over to Dad.

As he crossed his fingers and squeezed his eyes shut, hoping for good news, I leaped off the stool and raced into the manager's quarters. I picked up the phone extension just in time to hear Josie say, "Congratulations! You got the house!"

I screamed! Dad screamed!

We thanked Josie profusely, then hung up the phones so we could call Mom in her room. I knew she was still teaching Math Cup, but she'd want to be interrupted for this!

"Mom!!" I screamed into the phone. "We got the house!!!"

Five minutes later, Mom ran over with the entire Math Cup team. As we celebrated the good news, everyone on the team jumped up and down, including Lupe and Allie, their long hair flying.

"Is this really happening?" Mom asked as she jumped. "It's like a dream come true!"

"An American dream come true!" Dad added. I laughed. I could almost hear the eager barks of Comma, who couldn't wait to join in the excitement. "We can finally sit around the fireplace after dinner with a cup of chrysanthemum tea!"

"With Comma!" I added.

"And go to Home Depot on the weekends, for *ourselves*!" Mom giggled. "Buy all those nice fruit bowls and scented candles."

"And have barbecues and kick a ball around!" Dad said. He held up a finger. "That reminds me!" He disappeared into the manager's quarters and returned with a box, which he handed me. I peered curiously at it. A housewarming present already? When I opened it, I grinned from ear to ear.

Dad had gotten me very own soccer ball.

"I heard about you and Lupe playing in the lot, and I figured maybe you might like one of your own," he said.

"Thanks!"

"I know sports haven't always come easy to you, but I'm so proud of you for trying."

I gave Dad a big hug and thought about Jason, and how much it meant having a parent who supported you. All those years, when we didn't have the nicest homes, we always had each other. And that was worth more than gold.

"You want to . . . kick it around with your old man sometime?" Dad asked. "In our new backyard?"

"I'd love that," I said, and smiled.

CHAPTER 30

After Josie the agent told us our offer was accepted, we sprang into action. A million things had to be done before we could finally get the house key. A hundred pounds of paper had to be signed. The bank had to send special people to judge the value of the house. Then there were the inspections. In the middle of the chaos, I got another call.

"Mia! This is Mr. and Mrs. Wong over at Lotus Garden! You said to call you when we had an extra-large to-go order for dumplings from a hotel. Well . . . we have one!"

I gasped, gesturing for Dad to hand me a notebook.

"What's the name of the hotel?" I asked.

After Mrs. Wong told me the name and I jotted it down, I thanked her. Turning to my dad, I cried, "Drop your escrow papers! I found the Chinese soccer team! They're at the Ambrose! Let's go!"

. . .

The Ambrose was a small, modern hotel in the heart of Pasadena. Stepping inside, I saw they had a giant ceramic rose encased in glass at the front desk. I wondered if it was a nod to the Rose Bowl. Lupe smiled when she saw it too. I'd asked her and Jason to come along.

"Whoaaa," Lupe said, walking toward the rose, but I pulled her back.

"Remember what happened the last time we went to another hotel's front desk?" I led her to the seats by the fireplace instead.

We all sat on a couch, wriggling impatiently. Lupe looked down at the math papers she'd brought along with her, but none of us could concentrate on anything. We were all dying to ask the soccer players our own questions. Jason wanted to know how they got past their parents' advice and comments. Lupe wanted to know how they got past all the stereotypes of what girls were "supposed to do."

And I wanted to know if they were proud to be playing in America because it's America, or proud to be trailblazers because they're Chinese. I leaned against my soccer ball, which I'd brought along with me. If it were me, I'd definitely feel both. I stared into the fireplace as we waited, mesmerized by the moving embers. What was it about the moving flames that made Dad feel like we'd arrived? Was it the warm glow? Or the crackling sound?

I closed my eyes, imagining a popcorn of dreams was coming true in our new fireplace.

"Whatcha thinking about?" Lupe asked, looking up from her math.

"Our new house." I turned to Dad and asked, "When are we going to get it? Why do we have to wait?" I could hear Comma's whimpers in my head. I imagined him curling up by my feet in front of our future fireplace.

"They have to do all the inspections, and that takes a little bit of time."

Lupe reached out a hand to the fire, feeling the warmth. "Just think—we can finally make s'mores over Christmas!"

I smiled, then remembered—"*If* I get in, I'll be in San Francisco."

"You *will* get in," Lupe said.

"It's, like, crazy competitive," I reminded her.

"Not as competitive as Math Cup." She took out the crinkled worksheet, and I leaned over. It was like reading a foreign language. "This is only a fraction of what we have to know," she said. "The Sentilla Beach team, they don't even need these worksheets. They already have 'em in their head."

"So?" I asked. "It's not what you know; it's how you use it."

"Well, they use it in half the time."

"If they're rushing, they'll make mistakes," I insisted. I glanced over at the elevators. Still no sign of the soccer team.

"That's what Allie was saying too!" she said. "I really want us to win so the boys can see it's possible. That girls can kick butt at math. We don't have to just be the butt of their tennis jokes."

"Tennis jokes?"

Lupe rolled her eyes and asked, "What do you call a girl who stands in the middle of a tennis court?"

"What?" Jason and I said.

"Annette."

Jason threw his head back and laughed so hard, the flames in the fireplace shook. I rolled my eyes with Lupe.

Then we heard a *ding* and the elevator doors opened. I turned around and spotted a middle-aged Asian man in a gray blazer and nylon sweatpants. I nudged Jason, and he quieted down.

"You think he's with them?" Lupe asked.

"Could be! Look at those sweats!" I exclaimed.

I sprang up and walked over to him. "Excuse me, I'm sorry to bother you," I said. "But would you happen to know the Chinese women's soccer team?"

The man in the gray blazer looked me up and down. "Who are you?" he inquired in Chinese.

I stood up tall and replied in Chinese, "I'm Mia Tang. I'm a student journalist, and I'd love to speak to them!"

He took a seat in one of the empty chairs next to the fireplace and reached for a newspaper, holding it in front of his face. "You have the wrong hotel," he said.

"Are you . . . their coach?" I asked, taking a wild guess.

He didn't respond for so long, I worried my question had gotten lost in a crossword puzzle.

"Yes," he finally admitted. "But they're *not* here."

Hope flooded inside me.

"It's so great to meet you . . . Mr. . . . ?"

"Lu," he supplied.

I grabbed his hand away from the newspaper and started shaking it. "Do you know where I could find them? I just need a couple of minutes of their—"

"They're not taking any interviews," he said, finally putting the paper down and studying me. "Especially not from a *student* journalist."

I felt my cheeks heating up like the fireplace. I glanced over at Lupe, and she mouthed, *Don't give up!*

"Actually," I tried again, "I'm a journalist who happens to be a student. I write for all kinds of newspapers! Here, I can show you—"

I started digging out my columns from my backpack, but he waved me off. "They're staying focused on the big game—that's where their heads are at."

"And I totally get that! This game is so important—to Chinese girls all over, actually, which is why I want to speak to them. I just want to find out about their journey, how they overcame the obstacles to get here."

Mr. Lu shook his head hard, like he was trying to air-dry his hair.

"But the world needs to hear their story!" I cried.

"The world needs them to *win*," Coach Lu said. "Then they'll want to hear their story. They'll see it's possible for all girls. Not just girls with platinum sponsorships, gracing the cover of *Sports Illustrated*. These women worked their butts off to get to this moment. And I won't have them distracted."

The elevator doors *ding*ed open again, and a chorus of laughter and Mandarin came gushing out. Hearing my mother tongue, I turned and gasped. There they were! The Chinese players!

"Sun Wen!" I cried, running up to the famous striker and captain of the team. "Hi! It's such an honor to meet you! You too, Gao Hong!"

I called out to them in Mandarin like I knew them. Like they were my sisters. Because that's how it felt. Their jet-black hair was straight and silky like mine, and their almond-shaped eyes smiled back at me, curious.

"My name is Mia Tang and I'm a writer and I'd love to interview you! Just five minutes! I've been to every hotel and noodle place in Pasadena looking for you guys!"

Coach Lu dashed over, trying to sandwich himself between me and the players.

"Ignore her," he told them. "She's just a kid."

Sun Wen raised an eyebrow at her coach.

"I was just a kid too when I moved away to play soccer at a special school. About your age." She smiled at me, then looked around to her fellow players. "What do you say, ladies? We got five minutes for 'just a kid'?"

Gao Hong, the goalie, reached for my soccer ball and started spinning it with her finger.

"We got fifteen!" she cried, then leaned over and asked, "You hungry? I heard the doughnuts in America are pretty amazing."

"I love doughnuts!" Jason declared. I turned to him, surprised he could understand Mandarin, but he followed just fine. As I translated for Lupe what Gao said, we led the players over to the hotel coffee shop for some piping-hot American doughnuts!

CHAPTER 31

Over doughnuts and lemonade, I fired away with all my questions.

"Is it true you used to work in a factory?" I asked Gao Hong.

"Yes," she said. "I didn't start playing until I was eighteen. My boss said I should play for the factory team."

I scribbled this down on my reporter's notepad.

"Soccer chose me, not the other way around," she added with a chuckle.

"Was it hard? Going from working at a factory to playing at the international level?" I asked.

"Very," Gao said. "The other factory workers all thought I was insane. But I loved the sport. Sometimes my voice was the only one cheering me on. Other times, my voice was the loudest one doubting myself."

"I can relate so hard," Lupe said when I translated for her. "So how'd you conquer it?"

"I listened to my inner coach, and I ignored my inner enemy," Gao replied with a smile. "The toughest opponent is always yourself."

I jotted the wise words down. It was so true. I stared at the soccer ball in Gao's hand, thinking of all the times I'd chickened out in class. Not because of Bethany Brett or Mr. Antwell . . . but because of me, and the little voice in my head.

"But it's not so easy when you're little," Sun Wen, the captain, chimed in. She told us she left home at the age of ten to attend a soccer school.

"You were only *ten*??" I exclaimed.

Sun Wen nodded.

"What about your parents?" I asked. "Did you miss them?"

"I did. Especially my father," she said. "Most fathers in China cannot accept girls playing soccer. It's the culture. Girls are supposed to be shy and steady. But my dad, he urged me to try."

"What a great guy," Jason said, putting his doughnut down.

"But when I was fourteen," she went on, "I had a coach at the sports school who said, 'You will never be a good soccer player. You should stop.'"

We all gasped. Jason's hands fisted into small, angry soccer balls. My mind immediately went back to all the people who told me I couldn't achieve my writing dreams—that I wasn't good enough, that I couldn't make it. Even my own mother had her doubts in the beginning. The scar of their words still hurt sometimes.

"So what'd you do?" I asked.

"I worked harder," Sun Wen explained. "I wanted to prove him wrong. There was not one iota of a chance I was going to let him win."

I put my pen down and pumped my arm in the air. "You go, girl! Now you're going to the World Cup!"

"And we're going to get that Cup!" The captain turned to her teammates. "Right, ladies?"

They whooped with joy.

Liu Ailing, one of the midfielders, told us that beyond just the honor of winning, they and their families were counting on the money.

Many of them had a meager salary, even now. Unlike the US team, they didn't have splashy sponsorships and mega cash coming in. But if they won the World Cup, they could get $10,000 per player.

Hearing that, I immediately put my doughnut back. But Sun Wen chuckled and assured me that Adidas was covering their hotel expenses, thankfully.

"The point is, we have clawed our way here, fought tooth and nail to get out of poverty, the factories, and, most of all, the loud skepticism of naysayers," Sun Wen said. "The future of Chinese girls depends on us. We want to show the world we can be active. We can be anything!"

"YESSSSS!!!" I shouted, raising my lemonade. Suddenly, I realized that tears were streaming down my cheeks.

It was Jason who asked a final question as we all walked out of the restaurant. He wanted to know the team's favorite food.

The women responded in unison, "Roasted Peking duck!"

CHAPTER 32

My smile was as wide as the sun as we left the hotel. Seeing people who looked like me, spoke the same language, liked the same *food* as me, all fighting for the same dreams—it was the most validating experience ever.

"I don't know about you, but I feel like I'm on fire!" Lupe said, skipping in the parking lot toward Dad's car. He had gone to drop off the signed papers for the house at Josie's office while we were interviewing the players.

Breathlessly, I told Dad everything. "They were amazing! They told us all about what it was like for them growing up and how sometimes even their own coaches didn't believe in them, how they kept hustling and fighting for their dream!"

Dad laughed. "Sounds like someone I know," he said with a wink.

"Can't wait to get home and write this up!"

"I can't wait to call up Allie! She'll be so psyched!" Lupe said. "*And* after what I just heard, Sentilla better watch out!"

"Hey, you think they'd be into trying some American roast duck??" Jason mused.

"If you make it!" I clapped my hands. "But you'll have to come back to the restaurant. No way can you roast a duck in our tiny kitchen."

"I'll think about it," Jason said.

I turned back to Dad. "So how was Josie? Everything okay with the house?"

"Great! They're doing the inspection tomorrow!"

I breathed in this moment. I couldn't believe we were actually here, steps away from getting the house! My mind flashed with all the times my mom and I would peer into big American homes on Meadow Lane. We were outsiders looking in. Just like the brave Chinese soccer players. They were outsiders too, and now look—they were here, in Pasadena, about to play one of the biggest matches in the world!

In that moment, I knew who I was cheering for.

CHAPTER 33

That night, I stayed up late working on my article about the Chinese soccer players and their heroic struggle.

For striker and captain Sun Wen, it wasn't easy getting to the World Cup. At the young age of ten, she moved away from home to attend a sports school. And for goalie Gao Hong, the first time she touched a soccer ball was when she was an eighteen-year-old factory worker. Women's soccer wasn't as prevalent or even approved of in Chinese culture in those days. As Sun pointed out, girls were traditionally expected to be "shy and steady." This year's World Cup proves to a country that once did not think women were good enough that girls can do anything. Indeed, if the Chinese team wins, it would be a milestone for not just China but all of womankind! And this Chinese American reporter is thrilled to be cheering for Team China!

My eyes watered as I thought back to all the times my lao lao offered my cousin Shen more shrimp just because he's a boy, or my nai nai commented that I shouldn't be so loud because I was a girl. I thought about Lupe, who, despite being the most brilliant mathematician on the team, still had to put up with ridiculous tennis jokes from the boys.

They were pesky, pebbly little comments, and we ignored them all the time. But over the years, the pebbles became boulders.

It must have been so hard for the Chinese women to play with so many boulders in their path. But every time the Chinese women scored, a little piece of the rock chipped away. I smiled, holding my article to my chest. I wanted the players to read it—I'd have to send it to them!

What had started out as a way to improve my PE grade had become so much more. Mr. Antwell was right: A thousand words was so much richer than a picture. And soccer was so much more than just kicking a ball around. I was glad he pushed me not to give up.

I put my article in my backpack. Changing into my pajamas, I reached for one more diary entry from Michael Yao and got into bed.

Dear diary,
Now that I'm a junior, I'm starting to think about college. I really want to pursue music and go to the Berklee College of Music. According to my band teacher, Berklee's the best for trumpet. Mr. B says I have potential because I have good air. (Ha! All I have to do is close my eyes, picture some racist customers, and boom, instant hot air!)

In all seriousness, I'd like to go to Berklee so I can learn from the best. I want to play on the streets of Boston and study abroad in Valencia, Spain. I want to go to Berklee so I can be <u>me</u>.

When I told Dad I was thinking about Berklee, he got all excited. He thought I meant UC Berkeley, as in the Bay Area. He said that's great—UCs are cheap and I can come down on weekends to help him and Mom with the restaurant.

I told him that's exactly what I'm <u>not</u> doing. It's why I'm choosing Berklee in Boston, so I can be far, far away. I have no intention of helping with the family business.

Dad didn't take that so well. He threatened to cut me off and not pay a cent for my school. Music is not a "real" profession, he says. There are too many players, and I'll just end up a homeless person begging for a quarter in a hat.

I don't care what he says, <u>I am getting out of here even if it kills me.</u>

Michael Yao

P.S. What if Dad's right? What if I go all

the way to Boston and find out I don't
have what it takes to be in the big leagues?

WHOA.

I jumped out of bed and went to the phone, tempted to call
Mr. Yao. I wanted to know what college he actually went to. But it
was already 10:00.

I got back in bed and decided that I'd ask him tomorrow. Even if
it was scary, and even if he didn't want to talk about it, I'd dig and
dig—*because I, Mia Tang, am a journalist.* I'd proved it today, at the
hotel. And I wouldn't give up until I got an answer out of the grown-
up Michael Yao.

I closed my eyes.

And I wished with all my might that Mr. Yao went to Boston.

CHAPTER 34

The shrill of the telephone woke me up the Monday of Lupe's first Math Cup competition. I wasn't surprised to hear her voice, but I didn't expect her to blurt, "Have you seen the headline?"

I reached for the latest *LA Times* and turned to the Sports section as she told me to do.

The headline read: "Don't Even Think About It!" It went on to describe the consequences if Team China won the match.

"'What happens to the future of American soccer, the endorsement-earning power of the US midfielder, and for heaven's sake, Soccer Barbie if the United States can't find a way to prevent China's dangerous Sun Wen from finding the upper corner?'" I read aloud. My cheeks burned.

"Soccer Barbie??" Lupe and I blurted out at the same time, offended.

"And '*dangerous*' Sun Wen?" I added.

"You should have seen the headline from the *LA Post* today," Lupe said. "It read 'China Must Be Stopped!'"

I frowned. "Why do they have to frame it like that? Can't we just celebrate all the players as impressive, kick-butt women? And who cares how many Soccer Barbies get sold?" I fumed.

Yesterday's paper was still on the table too, and I noticed another headline: "Success of the Women's World Cup Is . . . Looking Good."

"Ugh! And there's this!" I said to Lupe, reading to her again. The article was talking about Team USA's appearance on *The Late Show with David Letterman.*

"'Letterman, who could no longer bottle his enthusiasm for Chastain and her US soccer teammates, said last night, "The US team—and this may come out wrong, but I'll just say it now—is Babe City, ladies and gentlemen. Babe City!"'"

I threw the paper down, disgusted.

"I know!" Lupe cried. "Why do they have to say that? We work so hard but with one word, they can wipe everything out! And all that matters is how we look!"

"It's ridiculous! Even when we achieve the highest level of sports achievements!" I said.

Lupe and I were both furious. We were Team USA when they were being objectified in the press, and we were Team China when they were being attacked.

We stayed on the phone while we got ready for school, and I told Lupe to put all this aside, not even think about it, and just focus on her competition after school.

"Are you nervous?" I asked.

Lupe took a deep breath. "A little—okay, a *lot*."

"You got this!"

"Thanks. I'm feeling good."

"Did you tell Allie about the interview?"

"Yeah!" Lupe said. Then, in a small voice, she asked, "Hey, Mia? How do you know if you like someone?"

I thought about the question. "It's like you said before. You get a volcano-y feeling inside when you're around them." I felt warm just saying the words, even though I no longer liked Da-Shawn. Maybe it was impossible to cool *all* the lava.

"What if you just look at them a lot?" Lupe asked.

"That counts too, I think. Doesn't have to be a volcano. Could also be a sunset. Why? You like someone?"

There was a long pause on the other line. It wasn't *Jason*, was it? Finally, Lupe whispered the name, and I smiled.

"But I can't tell if I *like* Allie because she's awesome," she went on, "or I'm just really excited because she's awesome."

"She does sound pretty awesome," I said. "Have you told her?"

"Oh, no, I could never."

I almost dropped the phone. *"Never?"*

"I don't know. We're on the same team. It'd be super awkward."

I nodded. It was so scary to confess my feelings to Da-Shawn last year. But look at us now, still working side by side together, editors and friends. When I reminded Lupe of that, she said it wasn't the same.

"Why not?"

"Because Da-Shawn's a boy."

"So?"

"So it's different." Lupe sighed. "If I tell Allie, I'd be telling her *two* things. One, that I *might* like girls. And two, that I like her." She paused, and pushed out the next words with a labored breath. "And what if she has a problem with either one of those things? Then I'm in trouble."

I could feel how vulnerable and scared my best friend was. I wanted to jump into the phone and give her a hug.

"You know who *doesn't* have a problem with either of those things?" I said. "Me."

"Thanks, Mia."

I spun so the cord wrapped around me, giving my friend a phone hug. I imagined Lupe doing it on the other side.

"I'm still figuring it out," she said. "But I really appreciate the words."

. . .

Unfortunately, the mood that greeted me later in PE wasn't a warm hug, but a "Boo, China!!!" I stared at my classmates, all dressed up in #9 jerseys—Mia Hamm's number. They glared at me as I walked past. The *Los Angeles Post* headline flashed in my mind. It probably didn't help that I was wearing a red shirt.

Bethany Brett, with her hair swinging in a ponytail like Brandi Chastain's, hissed at me as I walked past, "We're so gonna whoop your butt next Saturday!"

I wanted to say to her, hey, it's not *me*. But I knew it didn't matter. In her eyes, I was Team China, and Team China was the enemy. Ignoring her, I walked up to Mr. Antwell with my article.

His eyebrows jumped in surprise when he read the title. "You finally tracked them down! I can't believe it!"

Jason jogged over to join us on the field. As he hustled past the long line of Nike jerseys, the other kids looked at him like he was Team China too. I wanted to hold up my hands—*truce*, okay?—but I knew in sports there was no truce, only winning and losing.

"This is incredible, Mia!" Mr. Antwell said when he finished reading. "Some great quotes here! Really impressive."

He handed me back the article, and I asked hopefully, "Does that mean . . . ?"

"Not only am I changing your grade," he said, throwing me the ball, "I'm making you goalie today."

I caught it and yelped, "Me?"

Mr. Antwell was already dividing up the teams. "Bethany, Joanne, Stuart, Roxanne, Chris, Jason, you're with Mia."

As usual, Bethany slapped her hand over her face when she heard she was on the same team as me. "Mia can't be our goalie!" she wailed. "She'll let every single ball in! She has the hand-eye coordination of a laundry basket!"

"Who are you calling a laundry basket?" I snapped.

"Just look at your arms!" Bethany said. "They look like two bamboo sticks."

I grabbed the gloves from Mr. Antwell. "Oh, it's on!" As I put them on and took my position in front of the scary net, I imagined I was Gao Hong at the Rose Bowl. I was in front of tens of thousands of screaming fans.

As I clapped my goalie gloves together, all my fears evaporated.

• • •

That day, I played for Lupe, who still felt like she had to hide a piece of herself. I played for my mom, who had to secretly coach her students because the administration said her English wasn't good enough. I played for me, having to put up with Bethany making fun of my body every day.

Throwing myself onto the grass, I blocked the ball with all my strength. I used my hands, my legs, and when that didn't do it, I used my head. I didn't care if I got hurt. I wanted to show everyone what this thin bamboo body could do.

As Mr. Antwell blew his whistle and declared us the winners,

I threw my arms up to the sky and sank to the ground.

"You were incredible!" Jason gushed.

"It was like something just took over me!" I looked down at my calves, still shaking under my socks.

"Mia, you should have seen yourself! The way you threw yourself on the grass!" Stuart chimed in.

I grinned and tossed a line in Bethany's direction because I couldn't help it. "Must have been my bamboo arms."

Bethany rolled her eyes and kept walking back to the locker room.

"I'm so proud of you," Mr. Antwell said, helping me up from the grass and taking the goalie gloves back. "You played with your heart, and you didn't give in to your fear." Then he put a folded piece of paper in my hand.

When I opened it, I saw it was a note to Mr. Ingleton, my counselor.

Please change Mia's PE grade to an A for last term.
She has blown me away with her effort. —Mr. Antwell.

I threw my arms around him. "Thank you!!!"

CHAPTER 35

I clutched Mr. Antwell's note for the rest of the day and finally walked with it into Mr. Ingleton's office after my last class.

"Wow," he said. "Must have been some game you played!"

"Actually, I wrote an article," I informed him. Smiling, I reached for my piece in my backpack as Mr. Ingleton put on his reading glasses. I noticed he had today's *Los Angeles Times* on his desk, turned to the Sports section.

"You interviewed the players?" His eyebrows jumped up, impressed. But as he read, they dropped again. "Wait, you're rooting for Team China?"

I nodded.

He tossed my article onto his desk with a frown. "But you're an American."

"So?"

"So, it's your duty to root for the US team in any sporting event."

"But the American team, they look nothing like me. And I can relate so much to the Chinese players' struggle!" I pointed to the first paragraph, where I wrote about how Sun Wen's early days.

"I don't give a pencil shaving about their struggle," Mr. Ingleton snapped. "They're still the enemy!" He leaned in closer. "Don't you see what this match represents? It's about the future! Who gets to dominate on the global scale! It's about good versus *evil*!"

His eyes bulged when he said *evil*, and I got a full blast of his peanut butter breath.

"I know it's about the future," I said, stung. "That's why I'm rooting for them, so that Chinese girls everywhere can feel like they can do anything."

"Well, they can't," he said, jabbing his desk with one finger. "I'm sorry, but they can't come to our soil and win. Not over our girls. It wouldn't be right!"

I got up. I'd had enough of this conversation. I shook my head at Mr. Ingleton, disappointed he couldn't see past "us" and "them," couldn't see these players for what they were—players. Individuals. Little girls who had grown up their whole lives being told they *can't*. But they kept going, fueled by nothing but the blind faith inside them. They had the same hopes and dreams as Mia Hamm and Brandi Chastain. The difference was if they got theirs, an entire nation of people would wake up tomorrow and dare to dream bigger too.

I reached for my article.

Mr. Ingleton held it back for a second, then handed it over. "Do the right thing and edit that piece."

"I'm not going to edit it!"

"Then you're a traitor. You want to root for China? Then go back to China!"

My face turned scorching hot as I turned and practically ran out of his office.

CHAPTER 36

"Mia!" Da-Shawn called out from over by the library. "You have your column for this week?"

My face still burned from Mr. Ingleton's words. I turned and quickly hustled the other direction, away from the News Room and toward the parking lot. I didn't want to talk to Da-Shawn. I didn't want to talk to anyone. I just wanted to be alone. But the words followed me.

Was it true? Was I a traitor for liking the Chinese team?

On Meadow Lane, far from my classmates, I let the tears fall. Quietly, I tried the word out on my tongue—*traitor*. I shuddered. It was so terrifying. It felt like everything I'd ever done in this country could get erased.

I hid the article underneath my jacket as I walked back to the motel. An hour ago, I was so proud of it. Now it felt grosser than the bottoms of Jason's wet boxes.

If this was the response I got from my own school counselor, what would my classmates say? I couldn't let them ever know how I felt. Even if it was my proudest achievement as a journalist, I had to hide this article with my life.

Back at the motel, I went straight to find Hank.

He was at his desk in the back of East Meets West, dressed in a suit and gathering up his recipes in a briefcase.

"Hey! How'd it go with Mr. Antwell?" he asked with a big smile.

"I got him to change my grade. But then . . . my counselor sort of said something."

Hank searched my face. "What?"

I glanced at some of the customers still eating, not wanting to repeat it. I didn't want the stench of my new "traitor" status to taint the motel.

"Come with me," Hank said, locking his briefcase. "I'm meeting my lawyers at the Pasadena Grill. We can talk in the car."

That explained the suit. "I'll be right there!" I ran inside the manager's quarters to put my backpack down.

Mom had left a note for me on the kitchen table.

Mia—There are Girl Scout cookies I bought from one of my students in the cupboard and frozen pizza in the fridge. I'm at the Math Cup with Lupe! Wish us luck!!! Love, Mom

Girl Scout cookies and frozen pizza—it didn't get more American than that. And yet, *that word* still sat heavy in my chest.

I helped myself to a bunch of cookies for the road, scribbling a note for Dad that I was with Hank and to keep an eye on the desk.

On my way to the car, I spotted Mr. Yao out by the pool. I ran over, still eager to ask him my question about where he'd gone to college.

Before I could say anything, Mr. Yao barked, "Where's Jason? I thought he might have come here after school with you." He was sitting on one of the pool lounge chairs, reading the local Chinese paper. I noticed the headline read, "A Chinese Victory on US Soil? Brace for Riots!"

"I think he went to the library to look up roast duck," I said, then pointed at the newspaper. "Riots?"

"Not gonna happen. The Americans won't lose, mark my words." Mr. Yao folded the paper and stood up. "It would be a major PR disaster—can you imagine?"

"I guess," I said. I didn't really want to discuss this with him. But I did want to ask—"Hey, Mr. Yao, where'd you go to college?"

"Why?"

"Just . . . I want to know."

He used his newspaper to shield the sun. "I'm not the best person to ask for college advice."

He turned to leave the pool, but I blocked his path. I wasn't going to let him off that easy. I might not be the most popular journalist at the moment, but I was still a journalist.

"Please? Can you just tell me the name of the town?"

With a long roll of his eyes, he finally replied, "Boston."

CHAPTER 37

Boston?! The fact that Mr. Yao actually went there both blew my mind and confused me to bits. If he got the chance to go after his dream, why was he still so miserable? And what was he doing back *here*?

"So what'd your counselor say?" Hank asked, bringing me back to the car.

With a sigh, I filled him in.

"He said *what*?"

"And he called me a traitor."

Hank hit the steering wheel with his palm. "That's ridiculous! You're not less American because you're rooting for another team. By his definition, we'd all be traitors for listening to the Spice Girls!"

I laughed. The guests in the motel were always playing the Spice Girls. I particularly liked the song "Wannabe." But suddenly I remembered that one lyric—"If you want my future, forget my past."

If I wanted a future as an American, did I have to forget my Chinese past?

Hank turned to me and added gently, "The whole point of sports is they bring us all together."

"Lately it feels like it's tearing us all apart," I said sadly. I told Hank about some of the recent headlines I'd been reading . . . and some of what the other kids said on the field.

"I'm sorry. Those kids have no right."

"I know they're just words, but they hurt so much."

"Of course they do," he said. "It feels like they can diminish you. Deflate you. Take away everything you've done, with just a word. But here's the thing. Joy is a form of resistance. Passion is a form of activism. And you're out there kicking butt every day, with your writing, your humor."

I smiled at Hank.

"Plus your kindness," Hank added, "and now with your soccer ball."

My mouth opened in surprise.

"Oh, I've seen you out there with Lupe. You got some moves!"

I chuckled.

"The point I'm making is, don't let this ridiculous counselor or *anybody* take that away from you. You're a winner, my girl. Not a traitor. And don't ever forget it."

I couldn't help beaming, endorphins swelling in me as Hank turned into the Pasadena Grill and parked.

"Now. Moment of truth." Hank exhaled, and I handed him his briefcase.

His lawyers were already outside the restaurant, waiting. They had driven all the way from downtown LA in their Mercedes convertibles and BMW 5 Series.

Hank took his time getting out of his small Honda. I knew he had a lot riding on this case, including his condo. But mostly, his honor was on the line. And he had no intention of letting the Pasadena Grill walk away with it without a fight.

"Ready for battle?" he asked.

I nodded, putting my war face on. "Ready!"

CHAPTER 38

The Grill was decorated with gold and silver balloons when we walked in, like they'd just had a massive party. A giant poster of Team USA hung from the ceiling.

The hostess led Hank's battle team, me included, into a conference room. A few minutes later, Mr. Wamble walked in with his own soldiers. As the people in suits shook hands, Hank and Mr. Wamble took their positions on the opposite sides of the table, staring each other down like two strikers ready to sink the ball into the goal.

"I'm going to make this quick," Hank started, kicking the first offense. "The recipe you stole is a trade secret." He opened his briefcase and pulled out all the legal papers that they were planning to file in court.

"If it's a trade secret, why'd you share with me?" Mr. Wamble asked.

"Because I trusted you! You misled me into thinking there was a chance we could be in business together!"

"There was. But your recipe, I'm sorry, it just didn't blow my socks off," Mr. Wamble replied. "Neither did you, quite frankly."

"What's *that* supposed to mean?" Now Hank was seething mad.

"It takes a certain type of person to make it. And in my experience, they don't generally take little girls to serious meetings."

"Hey!" I erupted. "I'm his business partner."

Hank's lawyer Jerry waved his hands, trying to get their attention. "Can we please get back to the burger? How do you explain the fact that you released the Crunch Burger just *days* after Mr. Caleb showed you his recipe?"

"The Crunch Burger," Mr. Wamble's lawyer replied, "is nothing like Mr. Caleb's burger. For starters, it has different ingredients. It uses a rosemary—"

"But the *concept* of crunch you stole from my recipe," Hank interrupted. "It's a complete rip-off and you know it."

"Gentlemen," Jerry said. "We came here on the good faith belief that we might be able to come to a resolution. But if you refuse to see how we've been wronged here, we'll see you in court."

Mr. Wamble's lawyer laughed. "Good luck with that," he said. "Even if you *could* prove our recipe is derivative, which it's not, you'd have to prove that it's a trade secret."

"It *is* a trade secret!" Hank said again.

"Then how do you explain the fact that a restaurant called Do Fu Nao in Beijing has it?" Mr. Wamble's lawyer asked.

Hank froze. Do Fu Nao was the restaurant we helped in Beijing. Last Christmas, when we went to China on vacation, Hank started a pop-up burger shop. The shop was a hit, and everyone wanted his saltine burgers. So when we had to come home to Anaheim, Hank left his recipe with the owner to help him with his business. But how did *these* guys know about that?

Mr. Wamble must've known we were wondering because he said,

"When you're as big as we are, you have friends all over the world. A restaurant partner of ours told us all about it." He shook his head. "Way to protect your trade secret!"

"That was with my permission—" Hank began.

"Well, that was stupid! You let your secret recipe out!"

Hank's lawyers shriveled to the size of their briefcases. I could tell from the looks on their faces that this was bad. Perhaps even *game over* bad. As they led us out of the room, Mr. Wamble leaned over and asked Hank, "In China, of all places. Seriously? What were you thinking?"

. . .

Hank turned to his lawyers when we got outside. "What's the next move?"

"There is no next move," Jerry replied. "You gave out your trade secret in China!"

"So what? We're not even going to fight this?" Hank asked, confused.

Jerry sighed. "It's gonna be pretty hard to argue in court that it was a trade secret when 1.2 billion people know about it."

"But it's not 1.2 billion people!" I argued back. "It's not like he published it! It's a tiny restaurant in Beijing." I suddenly felt immensely guilty. "It's all my fault," I said to Hank. "I shouldn't have taken you to China."

"I don't regret going for a second," he said, putting a hand on my shoulder. "It's *my* recipe. It should be mine to give out."

"You might as well have written it down on 1.2 billion Post-it notes and blasted it with a cannon," Jerry said. "Because that's what the court's going to assume."

I frowned. "Why?"

"Because it's *China*!" The lawyer gave me a look, and I flinched, feeling the shame of all his feelings toward my old home. One by one, the lawyers started piling back into their expensive cars. The last thing they said to Hank before they sped off was "We'll send you our bill!"

Hank's shoulders hung low as he crawled back into his Honda.

I couldn't believe the injustice of it all. The Grill got to keep what they stole. My friend had to swallow his grievance. We'd lost before we even started the fight. All because of people's conceptions toward China.

CHAPTER 39

We drove home in silence. Several times I wanted to turn to Hank. I wanted to suggest that we find new lawyers. That we keep fighting. But I knew how hard it was, reversing the headlines in most folks' minds when it came to China. It was almost impossible.

Dad was sitting in the office when we walked back in. His face was as long as Hank's.

"What's wrong?" I asked.

"The inspection report came back," he said, handing me a thick packet. "They found something."

"What?" I asked, thumbing through the pages. It was very long.

"Asbestos," Dad said.

"What's asbestos?" I asked Hank.

Hank made a long and regretful noise between his teeth. "It's this material they used to build a lot of old houses," he explained. "It's not harmful if it's intact, but if it gets in the air, it can make you sick."

"How sick?"

He exchanged a glance with Dad, then bit his lip.

"How sick?" I repeated.

"It can cause cancer," Hank finally said, then named some famous people who had died from it.

I heaved a sudden breath of panic, thinking of poor Comma lying belly-up next to the fireplace. I put the inspection booklet down, not daring to touch even *that*. "If it can cause cancer, why's it in people's houses?!"

"They didn't know back then," Hank said. "Asbestos was great insulation. The trouble is, if it gets in the air, the particles are so small, you can breathe it in without even knowing. And it's so sharp, it can slice into your lungs."

I felt like screaming. "But we can get it out, can't we?" I asked Dad.

Dad shook his head with a solemn sigh. "Unfortunately, it's in all the ducts and walls. And the inspection report said some of it is crumbling."

"Oof," Hank commented. "Which means it's already in the air . . ."

"So we can't even remove it?" I asked. No. There *had* to be a way! I rolled up my sleeves, ready to tackle that miserable old asbestos.

"Removal is *very* expensive," Dad said. "And dangerous." He turned to Hank. "How much you think that would cost?"

"Way too much. If it's in the walls *and* the ducts? We're talking tearing down the ceiling and everything, and rebuilding the house from the ground up."

My heart sank. "So what do we do?"

"I don't know," Dad said. "Let's wait until Mom gets home."

I grabbed his arm and begged him not to give up on the house. Christmases with Comma in front of the warm fire, smoothies with Mom at the kitchen island—we'd be giving up on all *that*.

Jason walked in as I was hugging Dad.

"Hey! Just popping in to grab a roasting pan for my duck—" He stopped talking and asked, "What's wrong?"

"Nothing," Dad said. Turning to me, he added, "Let's not panic just yet. We'll call Josie together after Mom gets home."

I nodded.

Hank gestured for Jason to follow him into the kitchen. "C'mon, let's find you a roasting pan."

After they left, I sat in my room, waiting impatiently for Mom. I glanced at my bedroom walls, pressing on the paint with my fingers, trying to smell if it had asbestos. Of course, I had no idea what asbestos smelled like. I put my fingers to my eyes, rubbing in the painful reality that after all those open houses and sleepless nights, after we *finally* found the perfect house, there had to be something wrong with it.

Why did it have to be *so* hard?

I reached for the stack of Mr. Yao diary entries, wondering if it was hard for his family to buy their first house. And how did they come to buy the Calivista, anyway?

Dear diary,
So Berklee is out. I got tired of fighting my parents about going to a music school, so I finally gave in. BUT they're letting me apply to Boston University, on the condition that I major in accounting, not music. I said okay, even though the only accounting I plan to do is how many M&M'S to sneak to band practice.

I figure once I get there, I can always change my major. The important thing is that I get out of here. If I stay here, one way or another Mom and Dad will wrangle me back into the family business, and that has about as much appeal to me as Jimmy Vanderbean's gym socks.

Even if I don't "make it" out east, at least I'll be with a group who cares about me. Who won't make me apologize even after someone's called us a horrible name.

My parents don't understand. Every day they look at me like I've gotten too Americanized. And a part of me feels guilty moving so far away. But I gotta make my own path in life. So I'm applying to BU!!!

Michael Yao

Mom and Lupe walked in as I was finishing up the letter. Lupe gave out a yelp so loud, I almost dropped it.

"Guess what??" Lupe exclaimed. "We won!!!"

My hands flew to my mouth, and I leaped up from my chair.

"Oh my God!" I cried, running over to Lupe as the rest of the Math Cup team piled in. We started jumping up and down, celebrating the good news. "What was it like? Was it super intense? I told you you guys could do it! Were the questions hard?"

"*Super* hard," Lupe said. "But we remembered what we learned in practice, and when we got in there, we just kept our eyes on the goal. Right, Allie?"

She bumped shoulders with Allie, who smiled shyly.

"Right!"

"You guys were pretty awesome," Ethan said, then corrected himself. "You girls, I mean."

Lupe grinned. "I remembered what Gao Hong said about not being afraid and pushing out the negative thoughts. And everything came together! It was amazing!"

I hugged Lupe, wishing I could have been there.

"I am so proud of you all!" Mom beamed, falling into my reading chair with a big, joyous grin.

"Team Sentilla was *shocked*!" Lupe added. She told me about their matching polo shirts, Montblanc pens, and alligator-skin backpacks.

"Alligator-skin backpacks?" I made a face.

"But I told Lupe, it doesn't matter what they carry or wear," Allie said. "All that matters is what's in here." She pointed to her head.

"They said it was beginner's luck," Ethan said, rolling his eyes.

"Beginner's luck my mop!" I exclaimed. "You guys earned it with your hard work and determination!"

"And with our amazing coach." Lupe raised her hand to high-five Mom. "Couldn't have done it without you."

Mom high-fived her back, then put a finger to her lips. "Remember, not a word to the administration. I'm still not allowed to officially coach you guys."

Allie and Ethan shook their heads, clearly annoyed by this injustice. As Lupe and the others went off to get cream sodas from the vending machine to toast their victory, I tugged on Mom's arm. I hated to put a damper on her celebratory news, but she needed to know.

"Mom . . . they found asbestos in the house."

"What?"

"Asbestos." I started explaining what it was and why it was so dangerous.

"And we have it in the house??" Mom made a horrified face.

I nodded. "And it's crumbling."

Mom jumped up. "Oh my God!" She went out to find Dad.

He was sitting in the dining room with the inspection report open on the table and his mini Chinese-English dictionary open to *asbestos*.

"Here it is," he said. His fingers ran along the page; then his face relaxed when he read the definition. "Oh, it's just *shi mian*. They used that to build lots of homes in China!"

"But we're not *in* China anymore," Mom reminded him. I furrowed my eyebrows. Wait, so if it was in China, it would be okay?

Mom clarified, "And now we know it's dangerous."

Dad closed the inspection report. "Well, what do you want to do?"

"I say we call up Josie and get another house!" Mom cried.

Dad gazed at the telephone with a reluctant sigh. I wanted to block the phone with my body—save our fireplace! Our kitchen island! Our American dream! At the same time, I was pretty sure asbestos wasn't part of the dream. I sat on a chair, wrapping my arms around my knees, wishing it were easier.

Dad asked one last time, "Is that what you really want to do?"

Mom gazed over at me.

"We have to," she said. "For Mia's sake."

Dad walked over to the phone. I had to look away as he made the call to give up our dream house.

CHAPTER 40

Josie the real estate agent did not take the news well.

"You're walking *away*?" she barked into the phone. My mom was listening on the extension, and I could hear Josie's voice all the way from my chair. I got up and walked closer.

"Well, on page nine, it says there's asbestos," Dad said.

"That's to be expected," she said dismissively. "I mean, it's an older property. Everything pre-'78 is going to have asbestos. You just put a little something over it!"

Mom was firm. "It's asbestos, not a dent. I don't think you can just cover it. The report says it's in all the walls and ducts."

There was a brief pause before Josie spoke again. "Listen, this might sound harsh, but in your price bracket, you're not going to get a perfect home. There's always going to be *something* wrong with it."

Mom sat up straighter. "I'm not expecting a perfect home," she said. "Just a home that doesn't give us cancer."

"*Everything* causes cancer," Josie fired back. "Walking down the street next to a smoking person. Not wearing sunscreen. Eating processed meat. *Life* is dangerous. Does that mean we stop living?"

Mom's frown lines deepened, but Dad jumped in to say, "I'm so sorry. But this is a lot of money for us. It's our entire life savings. And to put it into a house that has asbestos . . . We just . . . we don't feel right about it."

"Fine. You want to pull out? We'll pull out." We could hear Josie typing on her computer on the other end, and then she muttered, "I knew you guys were going to be difficult. My colleague warned me. He said, 'Don't take on new immigrants. They're gonna be a lot of work!'"

"*Excuse* me?" Mom shrieked.

"You guys are all the same. You only look," Josie said. "Good luck looking for another agent."

My parents hung up. "Well, how do you like that!" Mom fumed.

I knew she was tired of waiting, tired of getting scraps and told she had to live with it. Tired of being told that was the best she was ever going to get. Tired of feeling bad for wanting more and being told to be grateful. All she wanted was a cancer-free home, and even that, according to Josie, was too much.

Tossing the inspection report into the trash, Mom burst into tears.

Dad tried to make her feel better. "Maybe there's a way we can just . . . live with it?"

"No, I don't want to live with asbestos!" Mom shot back through her tears. "I just want to have a nice home so I can sleep peacefully. So Mia can write. So I can finally have some counter space to make smoothies, with Asian pear and tapioca. Is that too much to ask?"

Dad shook his head. "No, it's not." A determined look crossed his face. "You're going to get your Asian-pear-and-tapioca smoothie."

Gently, I put my hand in Mom's. We all leaned in for a group hug, imagining the day in which we could finally sip that smoothie in an asbestos-free kitchen. Hoping our house was still out there for us, somewhere, and we still had a chance.

. . .

"Jason?" I called, stepping into the restaurant.

Lupe had gone home after consoling me about the terrible house situation. "You're going to find the perfect house," she'd assured me.

"My parents and I lived in an old shipping container in my grandparents' backyard until we finally found a rent-controlled apartment," Allie had added. "It took a long time."

"But what if we don't find anything? What if they're all bad?" I'd asked.

"Then you'll keep looking. And you're not going to settle until you find the right one." Lupe had smiled at me.

I guess we needed to be a little more patient.

"Jason? You there?" I called again. I wanted to show him the diary entry I'd found after Lupe and Allie went home.

He wasn't in the kitchen. José was helping Mrs. Sanker scoop out her homemade ice cream for the dessert orders. Jason's apron was lying on top of the counter. I picked it up on my way out back. Through the screen door, I saw Hank and Jason sitting on two upside-down buckets. They were so deep in conversation, I didn't want to interrupt.

"I get it," Hank was saying. "It's why I went out to Pasadena, hoping for some closure. Some acceptance. Some acknowledgment. But the thing is, that can't be the determining factor of why you're cooking." Hank pointed at Jason's chest. "You're cooking because you love it, because it's what you're born to do."

"Thanks," Jason said. "Now, why can't my dad just say that to me?"

Hank threw a toothpick on the ground. "Sometimes, people just can't find the words."

"He *had* words. You should see the diaries he wrote when he was young!"

I looked down at the newest diary entry I had found. Jason was right. Michael Yao had all the words.

Hank got up and gazed out at the horizon, in the direction of Pasadena. "You know what I was thinking, when I was over at the Grill today?"

Jason shook his head.

"All I wanted was for them to make this right. It wasn't really about the money or having my name on that thick leather menu of theirs. I just wanted two simple words. But they just couldn't spit them out! Instead of *we're sorry*, they scoured the world looking for an out." This time, Hank kicked the upside-down bucket.

"What are you gonna do?" Jason asked.

"I'm going to cook, is what I'm going to do!" Hank said. "I may not win in the courtroom, but I'll win in the kitchen."

Jason held out his hand. "And you won't have to do it alone."

Hank shook Jason's hand. "I'm glad to hear you say it. We can't go about life waiting for folks to spit out the words. We gotta keep going. Especially you. You're way too talented."

"Jason? Your dad *did* find the words." I stepped out from behind the screen door and held out a new diary entry. "Here."

Hank went back to the kitchen to get ready for the dinner rush while Jason read.

Dear diary,

HUGE NEWS!!! All those hours in rehearsal paid off. Professor Taylor recommended me to study for a semester at the Royal College of Music in London!!!

Can you see me playing at Royal Albert Hall? Trying to distract the queen's guards with my trumpet outside Buckingham Palace? (I bet I can get those guys to clap!)

I never thought this would happen to me, but being in Boston, walking around Charlestown, hanging around so many talented musicians, not having the weight of my parents' restaurant crushing me, I feel like I can finally be myself! And it's made a world of difference for my music!

Mom did not take the news well. She told me London is full of bland food. I said I'll bring some hoisin sauce.

Then Dad grabbed the phone and said, "You think hoisin sauce is gonna protect you from the racism?"

I blurted out, "Well, you certainly never did!"

The call ended with Dad declaring he wasn't going to pay for my ticket. I said I don't need his money. I've been making plenty busking on the street here in Boston.

Dad didn't have anything to say to THAT.

It took me four whole hours of playing "West End Blues" to finally calm down after that call. Why can't my parents just be happy for me, for once? I don't care what anyone says. I'm going. Nobody's going to stop me from going after my dream. Ever!

Michael Yao

P.S. London food is not bland. I'm looking forward to eating fish and chips—in what other place is it okay to eat chips for dinner?

I pointed to the line *Nobody's going to stop me from going after my dream. Ever!*

Jason leaned against the restaurant door and murmured, "Wow. That's all I've ever wanted to hear from him."

I nodded, looking down at the diary. "That's all he wanted from his dad too."

"So why doesn't he say it to me?"

I picked at the apron tie in my hand, wishing I knew the answer. Up until now, I'd guessed that maybe Mr. Yao didn't have a chance to go after his dream. Maybe he was stuck here, which was why he resented it. But he wasn't stuck!

In the end, all I could offer Jason was "Maybe he will. In his own way."

Jason looked down at his apron in my hand for a long time before finally reaching for it. He put it back on.

CHAPTER 41

With Jason in the kitchen again, I could focus on my writing. I still hadn't decided yet what I wanted to do with my article on the Chinese players. I knew my column was due soon, but I still couldn't get Mr. Ingleton's words out of my head. So the next day, I called up Da-Shawn.

"Would it be okay if I got an extension?" I asked. "I'm trying to iron something out."

"Of course!" he said. "Take all the time you need!"

But the two halves of me were constantly vying for more space. I wished they'd both accept the other as here to stay.

"I'm sure you'll figure it out," Da-Shawn said. "Can't wait to read it!"

I promised him I'd get it to him soon, then hung up the phone. I looked down at my column. It'd be so easy just to erase the line that said I was rooting for the Chinese women. Take that out, and everything would be fine.

With a deep breath, I picked up my pen. I thought of all the years of hard work, all the insults big and small thrown at me, how long it had taken me to get here, to finally be accepted by my classmates. Well, most of them.

But if I erased it, would I be erasing a part of myself? Would I be erasing my past, my memories? Would I too be calling the game before it even began?

The phone rang. I picked it up. "Hello! Calivista Motel. This is Mia Tang speaking. How can I help you?"

A flurry of fast and familiar Chinese said, "Mia! It's Gao Hong here! Listen, I wanted to ask you something. We just got an interview request from a station called CBS. You know of them?"

"CBS? Are you kidding! They're one of the biggest channels in America!" I said. I couldn't believe I was talking to Gao Hong on the phone!

"Our manager thinks we should turn them down and just focus on the game. But after the interview with you, I don't know. Maybe it's time we tell America our story."

"It's totally time!" I cried. "It'd be so empowering to every single Chinese American girl in the country!"

"You really think so?"

"I *know* so."

Then Gao asked, "Will you translate for us?"

"*Me?* On TV?"

"It'll mean a lot having a young Chinese American there. And you already sort of know us!"

My heart filled with pride. This was such an honor! Still, I twirled my pen in my hand, thinking. A few minutes ago, I had doubts about writing down how I felt on paper. Was I ready to say how I felt on TV?

I told Gao Hong I'd let her know right away.

Mom and Lupe walked in as I hung up the phone. My mind was still spinning. I decided to wait to tell them about Gao's call until I figured out what to do.

"So, how are they going to celebrate your big math win at school? With a pizza party?" I asked instead. "I hope they do *something*!"

Lupe exchanged a look with Mom.

Uh-oh.

"They did something, all right. Mr. Jammer took all the credit," Lupe said.

"But he didn't even show up!" I protested.

"Ethan couldn't stand listening to him brag," Lupe went on. "So he told the principal the truth, all about the training sessions at the motel and the carpools to the competition. Mr. Jammer was furious."

Mom looked down at her math papers in shame. "And I was told I can't secretly coach the team off campus anymore. Mr. Jammer is the coach. Not me."

Reluctantly, she handed Lupe the giant stack of math worksheets she'd stayed up so many nights working on. "I'm so sorry. Hopefully these'll get you guys through the next few competitions."

Lupe took the worksheets from Mom with equally heavy eyes.

"There's gotta be another way!" I said, furious.

"I don't want to make trouble," Mom said. "Mr. Jammer is a senior teacher at the school. I'm new. I need this job."

The air in my lungs ran cold at the thought of my mom losing her job . . . and us losing our benefits.

Mom squeezed her eyes shut, and I put my hand over hers. I knew how much the job meant to her, how much she cared about each and every student.

"All I wanted was to help," Mom said, her voice catching. "It's not about the credit. I just wanted you guys to do well."

Lupe gave her a hug, and Mom said, "Study these worksheets. Everything I know, it's in there. You're in charge now."

Bravely, Lupe nodded, hugging them to her chest. As she stuffed the five pounds of papers in her backpack, I asked Lupe when the next competition was.

"This weekend," she said, looking as worried as I'd ever seen her.

"I'll come with you," I said. Mom looked up. "Hey, there's no rule that says staff reporters can't watch!"

Lupe smiled.

CHAPTER 42

"Nice of him to finally show up," Lupe said, pointing at Mr. Jammer. He was getting out of his Honda as we arrived at the Math Cup.

This time, the competition was in Sentilla Beach, and Lupe's mom drove us since my mom wasn't allowed to come. I took in the gleaming, beautiful architecture of Sentilla's high school as Lupe turned to her team members in Mrs. Garcia's back seat.

"You guys ready?" They nodded. Over the last few days, she'd really stepped into the role of being the team leader. The night before, she'd held an emergency study session at the pool and Allie helped her pass out worksheets.

"I'm so proud of you!" Mrs. Garcia told her daughter.

We got out and walked over to Allie's mom's car. Allie's mom was wearing her grocery store cashier uniform because she had to go back to work. She and Mrs. Garcia exchanged waves as she pulled away.

I held my camera and snapped a Polaroid of the team. I'd promised Mom I'd take lots of pictures. She was probably back at the motel, biting her nails. But I had faith in Team Anaheim. We might not be as fancy as Team Sentilla, but our leader had fire in her belly.

"Let's do this!" Lupe shouted, and everyone high-fived.

Mr. Jammer walked over. "How are my kids doing?" he asked,

then pointed at my Polaroid. "That for the yearbook? Ooh, take a pic of me and the team!"

Reluctantly, I held up my camera as Mr. Jammer smiled. He insisted I take five different shots of him with five different poses. I wondered if I could cut him out when I got home and paste in my mom's face instead.

"We better get you guys inside," he finally said, leading the way to the auditorium.

I followed along after the team, trying not to stare too hard at the fresh flowers—even nicer than the ones Mr. Yao got at Home Depot— around the tall, graceful columns lining the front entrance. The place looked like a museum, not a high school.

"You know, I almost took a job here," Mr. Jammer bragged to Mrs. Garcia.

"Really?" she asked, impressed.

"I mean, I interviewed," he said to her. "I heard the parents here go all out. Big, lavish Christmas party, presents, the works."

He gave a toothy grin to Lupe's mom, who grimaced and replied, "And I'll bet the coaches also show up to every team meeting."

Mr. Jammer ignored her and opened the double doors. I looked up at the rows upon rows of tables set up in the giant auditorium. The floor was so shiny, it looked like an ice rink. On each table, there were M&M'S and water bottles as well as freshly sharpened pencils and blank notepads.

One of the PTA moms walked over and greeted us.

"They wouldn't let us put out calculators because it's against the rules, so we figured this is the next best thing," she said, handing Lupe and her teammates packs of M&M'S.

"Can I get one of those?" Mrs. Garcia asked.

"Sorry." She frowned. "Kids only."

Lupe's mom looked down, embarrassed. Without a word, Lupe handed her M&M'S to her mom, then walked over to an empty table.

It happened to be right next to Team Sentilla's. The Sentilla Beach team was mostly white kids. They wore matching polo shirts and alligator backpacks, just as Lupe had described after their first match.

Sentilla's captain, a boy with gelled hair and glasses, looked annoyed. "Go sit somewhere else," he said. "That table's reserved."

"Really?" Lupe asked. "I don't see a sign."

"Yeah, well, it's our school." The boy pointed to a table in the back. "Go over there instead."

Lupe ignored him, waving over the rest of her teammates and settling in. "We're good here," she said.

The boy glared at her. "Are you sure? This is the *Math* Cup, not School Supplies for Inner City Kids. I know the notepads and pencils make it real confusing."

Lupe turned beet red. I stopped snapping photos.

"I know it's the Math Cup. I never forget a face I beat," Lupe said to him coolly.

I grinned at Allie, who also looked impressed. *Go, Lupe!*

"That was beginner's luck," the boy replied.

I looked around for Mr. Jammer. But he was all the way over at the snack bar for the judges.

Yes, they had a snack bar for the judges.

Lupe crossed her arms. "Well, it won't be beginner's luck when I beat you *again*."

"No way. This is our turf. We have the home team advantage."

"We'll see about that!" Lupe said as the judges tapped on the mic for everyone's attention and the Math Cup officially began.

. . .

As Lupe and her team hunched over their table, working silently, I walked around and took pictures.

Each team was given three sets of questions. The team that finished first and got the most correct answers won. The atmosphere in the room was so tense, I almost choked on a pretzel from the snack bar.

"Relax," Mr. Jammer said, handing me another pretzel as the sound of papers being passed back and forth filled the room. The team members weren't allowed to talk to one another, but they could pass notes back and forth. "The good thing about being the underdog is there's no expectations!"

"Except our own," I reminded him.

Mr. Jammer shrugged and asked me if I'd tried the cinnamon-sprinkled popcorn. "It's organic!"

"Don't you care whether your own team wins or not?" I asked.

"Sure I do," he said. "But you can't expect a fish to climb a tree."

I furrowed my eyebrows, trying to unscramble *that* one as Mr. Jammer went to get more snacks. I started walking back toward Lupe. Lifting my Polaroid to my face, I barely had time to snap a picture before I heard a *ding*.

"Done!" Team Sentilla cried.

Already??

I turned to Lupe, who looked similarly panicked. As Team Sentilla waved their problem sets confidently in the air for the judge to collect them, there was a collective groan in the room.

"How'd they finish so fast?" someone called from the back.

"Duh! We're Sentilla Beach!" their captain replied.

As the smug-looking team sat back and tossed celebratory M&M'S into their mouths, Lupe urged her teammates to keep working. I took pictures of them in their hyper-focus mode and prayed that all of Team Sentilla's answers were wrong.

Lupe, Allie, Ethan, Ben, and Noah kept their eyes glued to the problem sets, working as fast as they could, but by the time they were done, five other teams had turned in their answers. The lead judge tapped on the mic again to announce the winners.

"In first place, with a record-breaking time and *perfect* answers, is Team Sentilla. Truly a magnificent feat! In second place, we have Newport Harbor High School, and San Marino High School in third place. To everyone else, great effort and we'll see you at the next Math Cup competition!"

Lupe's head banged on the table. Team Sentilla's captain leaned over and whispered, "Next time try the Piñata Cup. I'm sure you'll win."

CHAPTER 43

"Hey!" I yelled, running over. "You take that back! I heard that!"

"They were like that all through the competition," Lupe muttered. She grabbed her backpack and headed toward the exit without even touching the free school supplies.

"It's okay, baby. You'll get it next time!" Mrs. Garcia said. She hadn't heard the rude comment Team Sentilla made.

But Mr. Jammer had. His head had jerked right up when that boy said *piñata*. As Lupe and I made our way across the auditorium, I waved him down. "You have to say something to those bigots!"

"Now, now, let's not get all worked up over one little comment," he said.

My nostrils flared. "A *little* comment?"

"It's a competition. Someone wins. Someone loses. Emotions run high. That's the way it is."

I wished I had Michael Yao's letter with me to show Mr. Jammer—you can't just let racist "jokes" slide. They linger and infect you from inside, like asbestos. But I did manage to say, "No, it's *not* the way it is!"

Lupe tugged on my arm. "C'mon, Mia, let's go."

But I refused to budge.

"What do you expect *me* to do about it?" Mr. Jammer asked, wiping the popcorn powder off his mustache.

"You're the coach!" I reminded him.

"Yeah . . . you're the coach!" Mrs. Garcia glared at him.

He looked over at Team Sentilla, triumphantly holding their trophy in the air.

"I'll send their coach a note," he said. "How's that?"

I shook my head. That wasn't going to cut it. I didn't want this resolved between two old white men, behind our backs. We were taking care of this right here, right now. I started stomping over to Team Sentilla myself.

"Mia, wait—" Lupe hollered.

I hopped onto the stage before anyone could stop me. "Hey!"

The Sentilla Beach team must have assumed I wanted to take their picture. They started smiling great big toothy grins, posing with their trophy.

I put my Polaroid away. "I'm not here for that. I'm here to tell you what you said to my friend was not okay!"

Their coach looked over at the team, confused.

"We were just joking around! It was nothing!" the team captain told his coach.

"You think racism is nothing?" I asked. I repeated to the coach what the boy had said. "And let me tell you something," I went on. "Words like that make you shrivel up inside. They make you not want to come back and do the things you deserve to do." My mind went to Mr. Yao's diary. Each and every time a racist comment was made, it left a scar on all of us. I narrowed my eyes at the team captain. "Is that what you're afraid of? That Lupe's going to come back and kick your butt?"

His face burned. "I'm not afraid!"

"Then why would you say such a cowardly thing?"

"Why did you, Jake?" his coach asked.

Jake looked at his coach. His face had *do I really have to do this?* written all over it. The coach nodded. Finally, Jake muttered, "Sorry."

Lupe looked up in surprise. It wasn't a trophy, but it was something. For Jake, hopefully it was the beginning of understanding that he had to take responsibility for his actions. For my best friend, it was the knowledge that she didn't have to suffer through things alone. When one of us got hurt, *all* of us got hurt.

CHAPTER 44

In the car on the way back to the motel, Lupe asked me how I'd felt, charging up to Jake like that.

I shrugged and said it was nothing, even though my heart was pounding and I was seriously worried for a second that Jake would use his trophy to push me off the stage. But I was so glad we didn't just let it go.

"You were so brave!" Lupe said. "I probably would have just left. . . ."

"Nah," Allie said. She was riding with us on the way back. "You're braver than you give yourself credit for. We all are."

Lupe turned to Allie and smiled. I rolled down the window, feeling the ocean breeze as we drove through Sentilla Beach. The truth was, I wasn't always so brave. I thought about all those times I just put up with Bethany's insults. Even yesterday, I was thinking of erasing my own words in my columns. All because I was afraid.

But reading Michael Yao's letters had stirred something in me. They were a harrowing reminder of what happened if we just let racism go.

I told Lupe about the entry I'd read most recently.

"No way, Mr. Yao really went to London?" She threw her arms up. We were all rooting for our favorite diary writer. Lupe started pretend-playing the trumpet.

Allie pantomimed playing a saxophone, and we had ourselves a little back seat jam session. Lupe's mom chuckled from the driver's seat.

"You girls are so cute!" She beamed.

"We're not just cute; we're smart!" Allie reminded her.

"And talented!" Lupe added.

"¡Sí! You are all that, and more!" Mrs. Garcia added her own drumming on her steering wheel to our band.

Lupe giggled. "I can't imagine Mr. Yao playing the trumpet in front of Buckingham Palace!"

"I know, right? But he did it!"

"Wait, so why'd he come back?" she asked, putting her pretend trumpet down.

"That's the million-dollar question," I said.

"Maybe he missed his dad's food too much."

Somehow I doubted Mr. Yao missed anything about his dad. Their relationship was even rockier than his and Jason's.

"When we get back, let's look through the rest of the entries together!" Lupe said.

I beamed. "Just as soon as I call Gao Hong back!" I turned and told Lupe, Allie, and Mrs. Garcia about the translator offer.

Lupe gasped. "So you're gonna do it??"

I nodded, and Lupe clapped excitedly.

I decided I wasn't going to let *anything* stop me from translating for my heroes on TV!

CHAPTER 45

Gao Hong was thrilled to hear the good news. "That's amazing!" she said. "The interview is at the CBS studios in Los Angeles, on Thursday."

"I'll be here," I said. "How's training going?"

"Pretty good! We've been watching the Americans. They're fast and strong. But I think we can hold our own."

"Do you guys need anything?" I asked.

"You wouldn't happen to know where we could get some good Peking duck, would you?"

I grinned. "As a matter of fact, I do!"

• • •

I could hardly contain my excitement as I flew into the kitchen to tell Jason.

"Are you serious? They want Peking duck?" He ran around grabbing bottles of dark soy and chopping scallions. "I'll give them Peking duck! I've been playing with the recipe, adding more light soy! And five-spice powder! We don't have enough five-spice powder!"

I giggled. "Don't worry. We'll go out and get more!"

"Get some more hoisin sauce too, while you're at it!" he hollered as I skipped out of the restaurant. "Oh, and, Mia, are you sure they're coming? It's not gonna be like last time?"

I knew how Jason had gotten his hopes dashed before. And how embarrassing that was for him in front of his dad. But this time was different.

"Trust me, they're coming!"

CHAPTER 46

Lupe hung out with Hank while my parents and I headed to the Chinese grocery store to pick up everything Jason needed. My parents were thrilled to hear about my translation opportunity, but Mom sat in the back, a little quiet. She was still processing what had happened at the end of the Math Cup competition.

"I can't believe he said that to her. If I were there, I would have really let the other coach have it. I don't care if my English not so good."

"Mom, your English is *fine*."

Mom shook her head. She still didn't believe me, no matter how many times I told her.

Dad suddenly slowed down, and Mom and I peered out the window. There was a *For Sale* sign next to the Maple Hills gated community sign. There must be a house for sale inside! But instead of getting excited, Mom slumped her shoulders.

"Not again," she groaned.

We were all a little house-shopping weary at this point, but Dad pointed to the sign. It read *New Town House! Open House Today!*

"Wouldn't have asbestos if it's new," he said.

I glanced over at Mom. "Should we go look?"

"If it's really new, I doubt it's in our price range," Mom pointed out.

But Dad was an optimist. I tried to steady my beating heart as he turned in to the gate. As he rolled his window down, which took a minute because it always stuck, the man at the gate asked, "Can I help you?"

"We're here to look at the town house."

"Oh, you'd have to make an appointment, I'm afraid."

Dad pointed at the sign. "But it says there's an open house today."

"Is there?" The guard glanced over at the sign, then finally pushed the buzzer and let us in.

Dad turned to me and Mom. "Here we go!"

We thanked the guard and Dad stepped on the gas as the gate opened wide. Inside, it was like a whole other planet.

"Whoa!" My hands flew to my cheeks.

Maple Hills looked like a totally different *world* compared to the rest of Anaheim. The grass was perfectly cut. The homes were brand-new. There were bikes on the lawns. The bikes weren't even locked; they were just lying there—perfectly safe and sound.

"I could get used to this!" Dad laughed.

So could I. I could see myself walking Comma here.

We drove by a sparkling neighborhood pool, and Dad's face tensed. He started calculating out loud how many hours it would take to clean a pool of that size. Then he remembered we wouldn't have to clean it—it was a neighborhood pool. We could just swim. *What* a thought that was. He relaxed.

His eyes turned into beach balls when we got to 4888 Maple Hills, the town house that was for sale. It was a gorgeous cream-colored Mediterranean-style home, with big, bright windows and a grassy lawn—perfect for playing soccer with Comma!

Mom jumped out of the car, and I could tell she was excited too. We walked over to get one of the flyers in the box attached to the front tree. She looked at the price.

"This is actually in our price range!" she shrieked.

Dad clapped his hands. "We could plant a plum tree right here," he said, pointing to a corner of the front yard.

"And I could grade tests right there!" Mom said, pointing to the patch of shade under a leafy tree.

The front door was open, and I ran toward it. "C'mon, let's go check it out!"

As my parents and I entered the bright, open living room, we looked up and saw a bookshelf. It spanned the entire wall of the room. It was like this house *knew* me.

While Mom and Dad went to check out the gorgeous fireplace, I ran upstairs. This house didn't have a loft or a built-in desk, but the bedrooms had a beautiful view of rolling green hills. *Imagine* the writing I'd do with a view like that!

"Mom, this is it!" I shouted, running down the stairs. I put my hand over my heart. It was just like Hank said. My heart, which had been forever pitter-pattering, had finally found the calm I had been searching for.

Mom and Dad were already two steps ahead.

"How do we put in an offer?" Dad asked.

The realtor, a white man in his forties who looked like he spent *a lot* of money on toothpaste and had a name tag that said *Dave*, put his hands up. "Whoa there, hold your horses," he said, chuckling.

"We've only just listed it. We have to let everyone else take a look too."

"Yes," Mom said. "But we're just saying we really love it! We've been looking and looking. *And* this is in our price range. What can we do to make this house ours, Dave?"

"Sorry, absolutely no offers accepted until after next weekend," the realtor said. "Do you folks have an agent?"

Mom and Dad looked at each other. "No . . . well, we *did*."

"And what happened?"

Mom looked down, slightly embarrassed. "It's a long story."

"Could *you* be our agent?" I jumped in and asked.

Dave wriggled uncomfortably. "That would be sort of a conflict of interest. But I'm sure you'll find someone willing to take you on. Now if you'll excuse me, I have to get ready for some other families." He gave my parents a polite smile. "But feel free to stay and get a feel for the neighborhood."

. . .

We sat on the lawn, watching as family after family came and saw our home. Families dressed to the nines. Platinum rings flashing. My mom didn't have a platinum ring. Instead, she had wrinkles from washing towels and ink stains from handwriting math worksheets for her students.

"What are we going to do?" Mom asked.

"Wait, I guess," Dad replied.

A neighbor taking out his trash waved at us. "Um, you can't sit there," he said.

We scrambled up. "Sorry, we were just looking at the house," Dad explained.

"I know, but you can't sit on it until you own it."

Mom blushed.

"Well, we'll own it soon," I told him boldly.

"You're buying this place?" the neighbor asked. He looked shocked.

I nodded confidently. I knew we hadn't started the paperwork yet, but in my mind, it was as good as done. I'd already written five books in the bedroom with the view and run around the marble kitchen island about eighty-five times.

"I'm Mia," I said, shaking my new neighbor's hand. "And these are my parents."

Mom and Dad smiled and shook hands with him.

"Derek Hall," the man introduced himself. He pointed at the house across from us. "We live right there."

"Nice to meet you," Mom and Dad said.

"Where you guys from?" he asked.

"Right here in Anaheim!" I said.

"But where are you *really* from?" Derek asked.

I hated getting the *where are you* really *from?* question. I used to get it a lot when we first moved from China. But it had been years now, and I was starting to wonder if I was ever going to just be from Anaheim.

"We're Chinese," Mom replied.

"Chinese American," I corrected.

"Really? We don't have a lot of Chinese living in Maple Hills," Derek said. "You guys would be the first ones."

"Well, we're looking forward to it." Mom smiled and pointed. "I can't wait to entertain our friends in that lovely backyard."

"Oh, there's a no-house-party rule in Maple Hills," Derek said. "Sorry. Housing association regulations, you know."

Mom's face fell. "What about tutoring students?" she asked. "I'm a math teacher over at the high school."

"Can't do *business* here," Derek said, sounding offended. "That's definitely against the rules."

"We're not *doing business*," Mom quickly said. "Sometimes I like to give my students some extra help."

But Derek just shook his head and started listing off some other rules. There were a lot! And then—

"Oh, and one final thing: no pets."

"WHAT?!" I blurted. He *had* to be kidding—pets were the whole point of getting a house! "I can't get a dog? But what about Comma?"

"I'm afraid not," he said. "If you get a dog, he could run outside and cause problems. He might jump on people and bite kids. I'm sorry. Those are the HOA rules."

Dad crumpled up the house flyer in his hand and tried to pull me back toward the car, but my feet weren't ready to leave the lush grass.

I fought the tears in my eyes. It was so unfair. The house was perfect. Mom could finally have her kitchen island, and Dad could have his fireplace. And we wouldn't get cancer from the house!

I wondered if the perfect house was worth giving up the perfect puppy for—and hated that I had to choose.

"C'mon, Mia, let's go home," Dad urged. "It's not what we're looking for."

"Maybe I can write the housing association a letter!" I said, my mind spinning. "Ask them to change some of the rules . . ."

"We can't make an offer on the *hope* that after we get in we can change things," Dad said, tugging on my hand. "It's too risky."

I knew Dad was right. Still, I gazed longingly at the lawn, feeling the pull of my dog and the house. And feeling sad that maybe both would have to stay imaginary for a little while longer.

CHAPTER 47

"Why the long face?" Lupe asked when we got back with the soy sauce and spices. Allie had already gone home and Mrs. Garcia had to go to a babysitting job, so Lupe was sleeping over with me at the motel.

I told her about the Maple Hills town house.

"Oh, that place is *nice*," she said, flopping down on my bed.

"Yeah, but they don't allow dogs," I said.

"Really?" She twisted her face.

"That's what the neighbor told us. Hey, has your dad ever been in there to fix someone's cable?" I asked.

Lupe shook her head.

"Maybe I could hide Comma! There must be *someone* in there with a dog."

"I don't know," Lupe said. "It'd have to be a really small dog."

I frowned. My heart was already set on getting a beagle. They looked so cute with their floppy ears. But they also loved to howl. There was no way I could hide Comma.

I joined Lupe on the bed. "Found anything?" I asked her, picking up the last of the Michael Yao papers.

"Just this," Lupe said, handing me a recipe.

Across the top in faded handwriting, it said, *Roast Duck—Yao*

Family Secret Recipe. I jumped up. "Be right back!" I cried, and took off for East Meets West.

Jason was going to lose his mind!

. . .

Jason's eyes jumped when he saw the recipe.

"Ginger, honey, paprika!" he said, licking his mouth. "I can taste it already!"

"I knew you'd like it! Lupe found it in the stash of papers from your grandparents' restaurant."

"My agong had skills!" He took the paper from me. "Can't wait to make this!"

I left Jason to his cooking. Lupe was still in my room, only now she was holding another piece of paper.

"I found this taped onto the back of one of the music sheets," she said.

Another diary entry! I sat down so we could read it together.

Dear diary,
Mom dropped the news on me on Sunday that she and Dad BOUGHT a motel. It's a little place called the Calivista, over in Anaheim. I was in the middle of practicing for my audition at the London Philharmonic Orchestra. Can you believe they have a scholarship program for underrepresented musicians? (Take that, Jimmy Vanderbean! They WANT Chinese trumpet players!) Anyway, when Mom told me about the

motel, I was surprised. Both her and Dad have enough spinal issues just from working at the restaurant. I asked them how they planned to run a motel too.

That's when they told me they bought the Calivista for ME. So I could have a backup plan, "in case the music thing doesn't work out." Can you believe that? They asked me again to come back and transfer to UCLA. I said no way! "And by the way, things here are going GREAT, in case you're wondering," I said to Mom.

And then I hung up. I sat there in shock, hugging my trumpet, as the London taxis beeped beneath my flat.

They bought a motel. My parents, who refused to spend fifty cents on a box of tissues, just spent $100,000 betting my music career would fail.

One thing's for sure. I am never going to that motel. I'm going to make it here, or die trying!

Michael Yao

Lupe and I looked at each other, stunned.

"He's obviously back here," she said. "Maybe he didn't get the scholarship?"

"With *that* kind of drive?" I shook my head. I knew from

experience, drive like that is impossible to smother. You can try to hide it, but sooner or later, it'll poke its eager head back out.

"Then why . . . ?"

Outside, I heard the loud booming voice of the real Mr. Yao. He was screaming about something again. It was hard to believe that the same harsh voice was the voice of the tender, sensitive musician in the letters.

I picked up all the diary entries that were on the floor and got up. Enough reading and guessing.

It was time for answers.

CHAPTER 48

"What are you doing putting the paprika in first? You should roast the duck first!" Mr. Yao was screaming at Jason when Lupe and I walked into the kitchen. "You're doing it all wrong!"

"The recipe doesn't say—" Jason stumbled, dropping the paprika all over the floor.

"Why are you making duck, anyway? It's way too pricey!" Mr. Yao complained.

Jason picked up the paprika. Wiping his hands, he took a deep breath. "Dad, it's for the Chinese women's soccer team. They're coming to the restaurant tomorrow night, and I'm making them their favorite—roast duck," he said proudly.

"You invited them *here*?"

I'd expected Mr. Yao to sound happier about it. He was so over-joyed when we told him Team USA was coming.

"Yeah!" Jason said. "Why? What's wrong?"

Mr. Yao started pacing the kitchen, grabbing at his head. "You know the headlines. You've heard the people talking. They're all cheering for Team USA! If we serve Team China, what are they going to think of us?"

"Uhhh . . . that we're a restaurant?" Jason replied.

Mr. Yao stopped pacing. "I think you should call it off."

"What?" I exclaimed. "NO!"

Jason was so seething mad, he dropped the paprika jar again. The seasoning spilled all over, even onto some of the cupcakes Carmela and Tanya, our dessert chefs, had just baked.

He pointed at the door and shouted, "I've had it with you! This is *my* restaurant, and I'll invite who I want to invite. Now get out of my kitchen!"

"Son, listen to me. I'm just trying to protect—"

"OUT!"

. . .

Lupe stayed to talk to Jason, but I quietly followed Mr. Yao out. He headed for the pool, where Hank was setting up for an evening cookout.

"Stop barbecuing! Will you go in there and talk some sense into Jason?" Mr. Yao yelled at Hank. "He wants to invite Team China over here! Turn this place into Paprika Loser-ville!"

Hank put his tongs down. "First of all, you don't know they're going to lose. And second of all, even if they do lose, who cares? You don't get to tell Jason not to serve them. It's *his* restaurant!"

Mr. Yao shook his head, taking his shoes off and stepping onto the pool steps.

"Why'd you invest in this place anyway, man?" Hank asked. "Is it so you can control him?"

My eyes widened. I got up closer and crouched behind a deck chair, listening.

"I was *hoping* he'd spend some more time with me," Mr. Yao said. "Appreciate what I have to teach him about running a small business!"

Hank snapped his tongs in the air. "Well, criticizing him constantly ain't gonna make him want to spend more time with you."

"I can't just stand by and watch him make mistakes!" Mr. Yao hollered.

I shot up from behind the chair. "You mean like your dad couldn't stand *you* making mistakes?"

Mr. Yao nearly fell into the pool.

"We found your diary entries," I confessed. "From when you were a kid. I know all about your music."

Mr. Yao hid his face in his hands.

Hank walked over. "You didn't know they were reading them?" he asked, surprised. "Well, I did. And you know what? I was happy for you, man. I was like, *Right on*, when Mia told me. But now it's Jason's turn. It's his dream. And you have to step aside and support him!"

"I'm his father. I can't just step aside while you two run off to wherever!"

"We're not *running off*." Hank rolled his eyes.

"I see how cozy the two of you are! You're trying to replace me!"

"I'm not trying to replace you!" Hank barked. "He's my colleague. My partner! And I love hanging out with him. But nothing's ever going to take your place in his heart."

Mr. Yao swallowed hard. I handed him a towel.

"But you have to cherish that position, my friend. Every day. With your *actions*," Hank added softly.

"My dad never did that," he grumbled, drying his feet.

I furrowed my eyebrows. "Then why'd you come back?" I lowered my voice too. "Did your music career not work out?"

Mr. Yao threw the towel down. "No." He exhaled deeply.

He shook his head and started walking toward the pool door, but I followed him again. *"Please,"* I said. "Just tell us."

Hanging on to the iron gate with both hands, he took another deep breath. "I came back because my parents died. It was the least I could do. This place wore them down. I tried to tell them not to buy it, but they wouldn't listen."

I put a hand over my heart.

Mr. Yao let go of the fence and buried his face in his hands, crying. "They had asked me to come back, but I was stubborn. I had worked my entire life to get away. I thought if I came back, I'd be chained to this place forever." His voice trembled. "And then my father had a heart attack."

I gasped. "Oh, no!"

Hank led Mr. Yao over to the deck chairs, sitting down next to him and patting his back while he wailed.

"He died in the operating room."

"I'm so sorry," I said.

"My mom passed away two days later. Died of a broken heart. She couldn't stand being by herself." Mr. Yao looked up at us. "None of this would have happened if I had just listened to my parents and not gone to Europe. I killed them."

Hank and I both erupted, "You didn't kill your parents!"

But as we tried to console him, I could see the guilt pooling. The pain must have been so unbearable all these years. No wonder he was so mad—he wasn't mad at us; he was mad at himself.

"If I'd just given up my silly dreams, they'd still be here," Mr. Yao said, reaching for his shirtsleeve and blowing his nose hard. I imagined him blowing his trumpet with the same force.

"Listen to me. They weren't silly dreams. They were your passion," Hank said. "Pursuing our passion is what life's all about."

Mr. Yao gazed down at his reflection in the pool. "Passion doesn't pay the bills. That's what my dad always said." He sighed. "That's why I always tried so hard, after they passed, to make every dollar. Can't go back in time and fix what happened . . . but maybe . . . if I can just make an extra dollar . . ."

Hank and I glanced at each other.

"No amount of money is going to bring your parents back," I said gently.

My former boss rocked his body, absorbing this bitter truth.

"But you know what can?" Hank said. "The love and support you give Jason. That's how you can honor their memory."

Mr. Yao rubbed his nose and muttered, "Not much there to honor. My dad fought me every step of the way."

"So," I suggested, "be the dad your father wasn't."

Mr. Yao looked up at me with glassy eyes. And I felt the thickest of walls come down, just a little.

CHAPTER 49

Mr. Yao left that day without talking to Jason. He said he had to go pick up something at Home Depot before it closed, and he took off. I hoped that when he got home, they'd talk.

As I passed by the front desk, I gazed at all the keys. Imagine hanging on to all that pain and guilt for so many years. No wonder it shriveled Mr. Yao's heart up like a prune.

Lupe was in my bedroom when I got back to the manager's quarters, pulling her things out of her backpack for our sleepover. I could smell the delicious aroma of Jason's practice duck wafting from the kitchen. It made my tummy rumble.

"Did your mom like Allie?" I asked her.

Lupe nodded. "I think so."

"Does she know?" I asked.

"Who—Allie?"

"No, your mom." I smiled, taking my Polaroid out from my backpack.

Lupe shook her head. "I'm not sure what to tell her. That I'm confused? I mean, there's no *news*. Allie's still just my friend."

"That's okay. I don't think we have to have everything all figured out before we talk to our moms." I thought about all the conversations my parents and I had had about their jobs, trying to buy a house, the motel. Grown-ups didn't always have everything figured out either, and that was okay too.

Lupe peered at me and smiled. "Yeah, you know what, you're right. Maybe I'll talk to her tomorrow. And ask her if, besides the volcano feeling and the sunset stare, there are any other signs you like someone."

I grinned at Lupe. "I'm sure she'll know."

We plopped down on my bed and started going over all the photos I'd taken at the Math Cup.

"Mia! Look at this!" she exclaimed. She held up a picture of Team Sentilla working at their table. I leaned in closer. That's when I saw it: a calculator. Not just any calculator—the latest, most state-of-the-art graphing calculator. They were hiding it underneath the table.

No wonder they solved all the problem sets so quickly!

"They cheated!" Lupe announced.

I jumped off the bed. "You realize what this means? We have to demand a rematch!"

"A rematch?" Lupe asked.

Mom walked in, and I dashed over to show her the Polaroid. "Look, Mom!" I pointed to the calculator. "Don't you think they have to give us a rematch?"

"A hundred percent!" she cried.

Lupe shook her head. "Mr. Jammer's never going to agree to that. He'll just tell us to let it go."

Mom's face hardened with resolve as she took the photo and put it in her purse. "Then he shouldn't be the coach. First thing tomorrow, we'll go to the administration. I'm not going to stop until we get what we deserve—a fair competition!"

I grinned. "Whatever happened to not wanting to cause any trouble?"

"After what happened to Lupe at the Cup, I decided there are some things more important than job security. Like being there for my students when they need me."

Lupe threw her arms around my mom.

"Hear, hear," Jason said, walking into the manager's quarters. We turned around to see him holding a platter with his gorgeous entree, roasted to perfection. "Anyone interested in a practice duck?"

"Wow," I gushed. "If that's the practice duck, I can't imagine how good the real one's going to be tomorrow!"

Mom and I set the kitchen table while Lupe called up Billy Bob, Fred, and the other weeklies.

That night, we feasted on tender roasted duck, a warm beet salad that Hank whipped up, and mashed potatoes with caramelized onions. The meat from the duck slid right off the bone.

"This is the best Peking duck I've had outside Beijing," Mom told Jason.

He grinned. "I'm calling it Anaheim duck."

Hank laughed at the reference to our local hockey team. He pointed to Jason with a bone. "We should send some to them!"

"To the Anaheim Ducks?" Jason asked.

My eyes widened. "You just gave me a really great idea!" I told Hank.

Hank chuckled.

"You think the Chinese players are going to like this tomorrow?" Jason asked nervously as he reached for a duck leg himself.

"They're going to *love* it," Hank assured him. "We'll set up a nice long table for them out by the pool!"

"Should we run out and get flowers like last time?" Dad asked.

"Nah. The food will speak for itself. And we're going to eat it family style," Jason said with a grin.

At the word *family*, I looked around the table. They were all my favorite people, the heart and soul and spirit of the Calivista. I never thought I'd say this, but I wished Mr. Yao were there too, feeling the love in the room. And I wished Jason's grandparents could join us. Despite everything Mr. Yao wrote in his letters, I think they would have been very, very proud of their motel. And especially of their grandson.

CHAPTER 50

At school the next day, I kicked the ball powerfully toward the goal, fueled by the fact that that night I was having dinner with the goalie of the Chinese soccer team! Bethany Brett was the other team's goalie this time, and she tried to psych me out by running super aggressively toward me. But I ignored her, took aim, and—

"SCORE!" Mr. Antwell screamed, clapping his hands.

Pure joy coursed through my body as I ran around the field high-fiving my teammates. The wind billowed in my shirt. I wondered if this was how Gao Hong and Sun Wen would feel on Saturday if they won. *When* they won. I'd faxed my interview to my editor in Beijing and tucked a copy in Da-Shawn's locker this morning.

Usually, after I turned in a draft, I had a million nervous ants marching around in my tummy. But today, I was at peace. I had written how I felt. I was proud of those women, and nobody could shame me into feeling otherwise.

Out of the corner of my eye, I spotted Lupe running over. She was late again, but this time it was because she was meeting with the high school administrators about the Math Cup.

"How'd it go?" I asked her as Mr. Antwell blew on his whistle for us to start another game.

"We're getting a rematch!" she said.

"Really??" I squealed.

"The school called the organizers. At first they said it was impossible. They just wanted to bump up the second- and third-place winners, but your mom—you should have seen her! She advocated so hard for us!"

The ball rolled our way, and we both rushed toward it. I wasn't scared of it anymore. I kicked it hard, and it went flying over to the other side of the field.

"Good one!" Lupe exclaimed. As we sprinted to the end of the field, she continued. "Your mom said the last Cup didn't count and we want a rematch! She was so fired up! And it worked!"

"That's great!" I pumped my arms in the air. We reached the other side of the field, and I got ready to take my position as striker.

"Oh, and we also told the administration we want Mrs. Tang as our coach, not Mr. Jammer," Lupe hollered. "They said okay!"

I stopped running and jumped up and down. "YESSSSSSS!!!"

Lupe giggled as she passed me the ball. I didn't even hesitate. I kicked it hard, and though I didn't score another goal, the sound of my teammates cheering my name made my chest swell.

"Go, Mia!" they cried. I felt a rush like no other, and I ran up and kicked again. It didn't matter if we won or not; the joy of *trying* pounded in my heart. *I can do this!*

Look, I'm doing *this!*

• • •

I rode the high of my goal on the whole walk home with Jason. We chatted happily until the Calivista came into view and Jason stopped.

Mr. Yao was waiting in the parking lot. Jason had told me his dad hadn't gotten home until late the night before, so they still hadn't talked.

"Hey, Dad."

"I came by to give you this," Mr. Yao said. He held up a wooden bamboo box.

Cautiously, Jason opened it. Inside was an old wooden knife.

"It's your grandfather's special carving knife," Mr. Yao said.

Jason reached to touch the beautiful wooden handle. "You kept it?"

Mr. Yao nodded. "It's yours now. And . . ." He took his time to collect his words. "I'm sorry for the way I acted these last few weeks."

I could see that the apology surprised Jason more than the knife. He closed the box and hugged it hard.

"I just wanted everything to go right for you," his dad went on. "It wasn't so easy for my parents, running a restaurant, and I watched them struggle. But as someone recently reminded me, it's your life. You have to do it your way."

I beamed at Mr. Yao, so proud of him for finally finding the words. Finally finding the courage. Finally finding the heart.

Handing me the bamboo box, Jason ran up and hugged his dad. I wiped a tear from my cheek.

As they clung to each other, Jason looked up and asked, "You want to stay for dinner?"

Mr. Yao hesitated. "I don't know. I don't want to mess things up for you. Me and my big mouth." He glanced at me, and I resisted the urge to comment.

"I'd like it if you stayed," Jason said, smiling. "Big mouth and all. Okay, maybe not so big tonight."

Mr. Yao laughed. "It's a deal."

CHAPTER 51

That night, we set up two long tables end to end out by the pool. Lupe and I made a green table runner from one of Mrs. T's scarves to make it look like a soccer field.

At half past five, two Ford Explorers pulled up. As Gao Hong, Sun Wen, and the other players stepped out, I hurried to greet them. I couldn't believe they were at the Calivista—like actually *here*! I had to restrain myself from screaming and running over to the desk to call my cousin. Shen was going to lose his mind when he found out who'd come for dinner!

Instead, I stood tall in my black leggings and crisp white waitress shirt. Tonight, I was Jason's maître d'.

"Welcome to the Calivista," I said in my most sophisticated maître d' voice, in Chinese. "Ladies, may I take you to your table? Our chef Jason Yao has prepared an exquisite meal for you tonight."

Gao Hong and Sun Wen grinned while Lupe ran inside the kitchen to tell Jason they'd arrived.

"You certainly may!" they said.

I led them toward the pool, stopping to introduce them to my parents, José, and the weeklies. Billy Bob held out his soccer ball and asked if they'd autograph it.

"Of course!" Gao Hong said in English, pulling out a Sharpie from her pocket. I was happy to see she'd picked up some English in her short time here. "You play?"

Billy Bob nodded. "The other weeklies and I like to kick a ball around sometimes. Just casual."

"I like casual!" Gao Hong flashed him a smile. "After dinner, we play you."

I looked over in surprise. Was she *serious*?

Gao passed the ball to Sun Wen, who started doing a forward roll in the parking lot. Billy Bob hooted with excitement.

"Game on!" he exclaimed.

Sun Wen scribbled her own autograph on the ball and passed it to the next teammate as we walked and Lupe joined us. When we got to the pool, I noticed Mr. Yao trying to slip quietly past, but I stopped him.

"Oh, and I'd like to introduce you to Mr. Yao," I said to the players. "He and his family were the original owners of the Calivista."

"Now I'm just a small-time investor," Mr. Yao said in Mandarin.

"As well as a very talented musician," I added.

"Really?" Sun Wen said. "When I'm not playing, I love to sing!"

Mr. Yao looked surprised. He followed her over to the table, where crispy mushroom spring rolls were waiting for us in the setting sun. Everyone took a seat.

"What kind of music do you like to sing?" Mr. Yao asked as he reached for a spring roll.

"All kinds. My favorite is 'You Gotta Be' by Des'ree."

"I like that one too!" I said, beaming at Lupe. "I especially like the part, 'You gotta be tough, you gotta be stronger!'"

Sun Wen burst into song, holding her chopstick up as a mic.

"'Listen as your day unfolds. Challenge what the future holds . . .'"

I bumped my shoulder with Lupe's, and we joined in. Soon everyone, even Mr. Yao, was singing along. My parents clapped wildly for us when we finished.

"That was wonderful," Mom gushed. "Sun Wen, I had no idea you had such a beautiful voice!"

The famous striker blushed.

"She's also a great writer!" Gao Hong chimed in.

Sun Wen started to shake her head. "No, no, no I'm not. . . ."

"*Tell* them!" Gao Hong insisted. "She writes poetry when she's not playing soccer. And one of her poems even got published."

My head jolted up. "Can I read it?"

Sun Wen chuckled. "It's nothing amazing, but . . . I do have to say, I am proud of the last line."

Lupe tucked her hands under her chin, leaning in. "How does it go?"

"It goes, 'Come on, girls, do not wait to follow your dreams!'"

I gazed around the table, at all the women pursuing their dreams. *Living* that line of poetry. It made my heart glow with pride.

"You know what I think? I think you could have been a very good writer," Mr. Yao told Sun Wen.

"I *am* a very good *many* things," she said with a smile.

I clapped. Great reply!

Jason walked in as we were talking, holding up a platter of the most beautiful roast duck I'd ever seen. We all cheered loudly, and Mom held up the Polaroid.

"Presenting . . . Anaheim duck!" Jason grinned.

"That looks *so* good!" Gao Hong said, rubbing her stomach.

We all leaned in to smell the succulent, delicious aroma. Jason carved the meat with his grandfather's special knife, then served the first slice to Gao Hong, along with some steamed pancakes and sliced scallions.

She took a bite. "This gives Peking duck a run for its money!" she declared.

Mr. Yao laughed.

"It's my grandfather's recipe," Jason told her proudly. He looked over at his dad, a little sad. "He can't be here . . . but I think he'd be proud to know you're eating his duck tonight."

Mr. Yao reached out a hand to Jason. "I know he would. And I'm proud of you too, son."

Jason's plate shook with emotion as Mr. Yao stood up and gave a toast.

"To family," he said, holding up a cup of cream soda to the players. "Thank you for coming to our humble motel and being a part of ours tonight."

Jason beamed, his moist eyes reflecting the pink sky.

"To family!" we all echoed.

CHAPTER 52

True to Gao Hong's words, after dinner, we played a friendly match right in the parking lot. It was the weeklies and guests against the soccer players, and boy, were we on fire!

As Billy Bob and Fred played defense against Sun Wen, Hank and I tried to dribble the ball toward Gao Hong. The guests screamed at the top of their lungs as they ran, bursting into hysterical laughter every time Hank tried to distract the players to get past them. Hank had some . . . er . . . unconventional tactics, like pointing to the laundry room, making owl noises, and walking like a crab.

I giggled as he moved. But *nothing* could break the razor focus of Gao Hong, not even the arrival of paparazzi! One of the guests must have tipped off the *Anaheim Times*, because about halfway through our game, photographers swarmed the Calivista parking lot. But Gao Hong remained as cool as a cucumber, dead set on not letting a single ball get through her.

"Aim for the right corner!" Hank hollered as I tried to shoot a ball past her.

By "corner," Hank meant the broomstick on the ground, which we were using as the goal.

I ran toward the ball and kicked. Gao Hong lunged with all

her might. Even without her goalie gloves, she caught my ball easily.

The guests erupted in thunderous applause, and looking around the parking lot, I finally understood the power of sports. Never in all my years of working here had I ever seen our guests so energized about something. Hank was right—sports really did bring people together. I wished Mr. Antwell could have been there to see it.

We all played our hearts out that night. And even though we didn't win in the end, it was the most exciting thing any of us had ever been a part of.

Afterward, Team China stayed late to sign autographs, pose for photos with the guests, and answer questions from the professional photographers gathered around.

"Tell me, why did you guys decide to play an impromptu match here at this local motel?" one photographer asked them.

"We wanted to get to see America," Sun Wen said. "Not just at the stadium, but *real* America."

"And . . . ? Did you like it?"

The players smiled at me, Jason, Lupe, and the weeklies.

"We couldn't be more impressed," Sun Wen said.

My heart swelled. I felt the two halves of me coming together.

"Thanks for filling my tummy up with home," Gao Hong said to Jason. "I'm going to tell everyone back in Beijing about your duck!"

"Tell 'em to find me at the Calivista!" Jason winked at Hank. "My buddy and I will hook them up!"

Hank turned to Mr. Yao. "And maybe you'll play a few tunes for us."

Mr. Yao looked surprised, but he nodded and smiled back at Hank.

"Mia," Sun Wen called, turning to me, "we'll see you on Thursday? For the big TV interview?"

"I wouldn't miss it for the world!" I promised.

CHAPTER 53

Our motel soccer match was the talk of my school the next day.

"You think they're going to win?" my classmates asked me in PE. "How was their stamina? I heard their striker's tiny."

"She's *phenomenal*," I corrected them.

When Mr. Antwell put me on the opposite team as Bethany again, she whined, "It's unfair! Mia's been training with professionals!"

"I thought you said they were trash," I reminded her.

"They are trash!" she shot back. "But they're, like, *professional* trash."

I rolled my eyes. *Whatever.*

"So what do you think are their chances?" Stuart asked me as we hustled toward the other side of the field. "I bet my cousin fifteen dollars they're toast. Should I change it?"

"Oh, yeah," I said. I leaned over and gave him some advice: "Never bet against a Chinese girl!"

I said it loud and clear so all my classmates could hear. Then I took off running full speed toward the ball.

• • •

The next day, I massaged my calves in the car on the way to CBS Studios. Now that I was putting more effort into my PE classes, I could feel my muscles growing. Dad drove while Mom gave him directions.

"Take a left up here!" she said.

Dad put on his blinker.

"You ready for your first Math Cup as the official coach?" he asked her.

Mom nodded, patting her bulky purse.

"Got all my pronunciation cards right here," she said. "In case the other coaches try to out-English me."

I looked over and saw the huge stack of flash cards she'd made when she first started out as a substitute teacher. She hadn't used them for a few months, but now she held the cards tightly, like a life jacket.

"You're going to do great, Mom."

She smiled at me. "I'm driving the team over tomorrow with Allie's mom. She's staying for the competition!"

"Oh, good!" I said. "I'm glad she doesn't have to work this time. Allie is so brilliant, her mom should see it in action!"

"And if those Sentilla people try any more nonsense, I'm gonna pull a red card on them!" Mom said, whipping out a bold red card from her purse. In big black letters it read, *UNACCEPTABLE!*

I gave Mom a thumbs-up, glad she was willing to call out what Mr. Jammar refused to even acknowledge.

Next Mom pulled her tumbler out of her bag and held it out to me. "Try this! It'll give you energy for the big interview. I made it with banana and coconut water."

I leaned over for a sip. "Mmm!" I said. "Very refreshing!"

"It's good, isn't it? Not quite a smoothie . . ." Mom looked down. "But it'll do for now."

I nodded. None of us had mentioned one word about the house since we left Maple Hills.

"All right, here we are!" Dad said, pulling into the CBS lot. "Are you ready?"

I nodded eagerly and opened the door. *No biggie*, I told myself, even though it was my first time translating *and* I was going to be on TV. *I can do this.*

As my parents and I hurried toward the building, I dried my sweaty hands on my pants. My mind started reeling at the thought of the many Chinese words I didn't know . . . all those traffic jams and word crashes in my head whenever I didn't know how to describe something in Mandarin. Was I *really* the right person for the job? Maybe they should have gone with an actual translator.

But I pushed my doubts aside as I walked into the studio and spotted the players. They shook their heads profusely at the producers, refusing any makeup. Gao Hong held up a hand, shielding her eyes from the blinding studio lights as she studied the set.

"Hey!" I said as I ran up to them. "You ready?"

"I dunno . . ." Sun Wen said. "You think this is a good idea? Maybe we can still back out. . . ."

They looked more nervous than me. And for good reason. I knew exactly the butterflies in their stomachs—they were the same butterflies I got whenever I wrote a really personal column. Or told Bethany Brett I wasn't going to put up with her calling me names. And every single time I ignored those butterflies and kept moving, the world had rewarded me in ways I never expected.

"Listen, it's just going to be exactly like at dinner," I told the players. "Pretend that's just a big chunk of cheese." I pointed to the giant moving camera. "Or better yet, a giant juicy duck!"

That got a smile out of Gao Hong.

"And pretend the interviewer is just one of the weeklies," I said.

"I love the weeklies!" Gao Hong said.

"Can we play the interviewer too afterward?" Sun Wen joked.

"Sure!" I giggled. "We'll use the camera lights as the goalpost!"

One of the producers, Tim, walked over and asked if we were ready. Mom whooped with joy when she saw who was interviewing the team—Liane Johnson. She was a wonderful Black journalist, known for her thought-provoking questions. She was Mom's favorite journalist on TV.

The hair and makeup person walked over again. "Just a touch of foundation? Smooth out some of those splotches of sun?" she asked.

Sun Wen reached up a hand to touch her face.

"That's just our skin," I informed the makeup artist. "We look great just the way we are."

I beamed at Sun Wen, who let her hand drop so she could wear her sun spots proudly. She nodded to her team.

Tim the producer smiled. "C'mon, let's go. I can tell this is going to be a wonderful interview."

He gestured us to sit on the couch. I sat closest to Liane, who introduced herself to the players as a big fan.

As the lights changed and the cameras started rolling, Liane turned to Sun Wen and began. "So. You're about to play the biggest match in women's soccer that's ever happened. How do you feel?"

Sun Wen replied in Chinese, and I translated with a thrill, "I feel like I can finally tell ten-year-old me, your dreams aren't crazy!"

Liane laughed. "They certainly aren't!" She leaned in. "Take me back to that ten-year-old girl. What it was like growing up in China?"

The women gazed at one another, nostalgia washing over them as they relayed their earliest memories and I translated. The producer was right. This was going to be a *wonderful* interview.

CHAPTER 54

Forty-five minutes later, Liane wrapped up the interview with a final question. I could tell she was riveted by the team's responses the entire time, as the players took her on a journey of what it was like growing up in China and how they'd reached this pivotal moment.

"And if you could say anything, what would you say to all the fans of the American team watching?" Liane asked.

Sun Wen thought for a second. Then she answered, and I translated, "We would say we're cheering right along with you."

Liane looked surprised.

Sun Wen continued. "No matter who wins on Saturday, it's going to change women's soccer forever. And that's an accomplishment worth celebrating in every language."

"And how do you cheer for someone in Chinese?" Liane asked.

"We say *jia you*!" I answered, grinning. "Which means 'add oil!'"

Liane extended a hand to the team as the cameras zoomed in on our faces. "Well, Team China, I wish you every success and hope you *jia you* on Saturday!"

"Thank you," the team replied.

"And that's a wrap!" Tim called.

We all let out a great sigh of relief.

"How'd we do?" Sun Wen asked me. I gave her two enthusiastic thumbs up as my parents came running over.

"You were all *terrific*! So honest and moving," Mom said. She was drying a tear that had fallen on one of her math pronunciation cards.

"Did I get all the Chinese right?" I asked her.

"You got all the emotions right. And that's what matters," Dad replied. I smiled and gave him a hug.

Liane walked over to the players and said, "Thank you all again for being so honest and real. Your journey and struggle are going to resonate with so many Americans."

"Really?" Gao Hong asked once I'd translated. "You think so?"

"I know so. You may be playing for another country, but we're all playing for the same goal," Liane said. "So girls like Mia can confidently say, *I can be anything*!"

I beamed at her.

The producer chimed in with a few words of his own. "I hope you consider a career in broadcast journalism, Mia. You're a natural!"

I blushed. "Thanks! I'm applying for a journalism camp for winter break. Up in San Francisco!" I started telling him how wanting to go to camp was how this whole thing had started. I'd never imagined it would lead to me being on TV!

"That's the kind of attitude that will get you far!" Tim said, pulling out his business card. "I hope you give us a call when you're ready for an internship with us."

I studied the card. "You have a 714 number too!" I exclaimed.

"That's right! I live in Anaheim," he said.

"Really?" my parents and I said at the same time.

Tim nodded. "Right over in Maple Hills. It's a new development."

"We know Maple Hills!" Dad said. "We were thinking of moving there. But the fact that they don't allow any backyard gatherings . . ." He sighed.

"Or dogs," I added.

Tim's eyebrows knitted. "What are you talking about?" He pulled out his wallet to show us a picture of a Labrador retriever lying on a green lawn. "That's my dog, Bandit. There are tons of dogs in Maple Hills!"

Dad and I looked at each other, confused. "But the neighbor we talked to specifically said no dogs allowed," I said.

Tim pointed to the picture of Bandit. "I don't know what to tell you. I've had Bandit ever since I moved there. No one's ever given me any trouble. In fact, they're thinking of building a neighborhood park specifically for dogs."

Well, how do you like that? The neighbor had been making it up!

"As for the backyard gatherings," Tim went on, "of course they're allowed. It's where I have my annual Fourth of July staff barbecue."

Liane looked over and added, "Which is the *best*."

I looked over at Dad, and I could tell he was wondering the same thing. *Why would the neighbor straight-up lie to us?*

"I'm sorry you guys were misinformed. But it's truly a great community," Tim added. "The last I heard, the house on the corner is still on the market. You should seriously think about moving in!"

The community did sound perfect, except for one thing. We were clearly not welcomed by everyone there.

"Thank you," Dad said to Tim, and we shook hands and said our good-byes. Then Tim said good-bye to the players and walked back to his office.

Gao Hong handed me an envelope. "Before I forget, these are for you," she said.

My eyes widened as I opened it. Inside were colorful tickets to Saturday's game. A single ticket to the World Cup was worth $200.

She'd given me *twenty* of them.

CHAPTER 55

"What do you think?" I asked my parents on the way home. "Should we give Maple Hills another chance?"

"It *is* the nicest house we've seen in our price range. And it doesn't have any asbestos," Dad pointed out.

Mom looked down at her pronunciation cards. "But will we feel comfortable there?" she said quietly. "Maybe we're better off buying somewhere where people don't lie to try to keep us out."

"But then we'd be letting him win!" I cried. It made my blood boil every time I thought about that neighbor. Why should that awful man get to live in Maple Hills and not us?

"Maybe we could wait a few more years and save up money. Move somewhere where everyone is kind," Mom said. "I'll prove to the administration that I can take on all kinds of additional responsibilities. Who knows? Maybe in a few years, I could get a promotion."

I chewed the inside my cheek, tired of waiting. Tired of the maybes. Tired of working twice as hard for half the reward.

"He's *one* guy," I insisted. "We can't let him intimidate us." Still, I wondered, what if there were others? What if they made up more lies?

"We'd be directly across from him," Mom reminded me.

Dad reached over and patted her hand. "We don't have to think about this right now. Let's just focus on the Math Cup and the big game." He glanced at me in the rearview mirror. "Show me those tickets again!"

I beamed and flashed the colorful stack.

"I can think of a few uncles and aunties who'd *love* to come!" Mom giggled, referring to our immigrant friends.

"Some weeklies too!" I added.

. . .

The weeklies were delighted to receive the tickets when we got home, as were Lupe and her parents, and Uncle Zhang and Aunt Ling when we called them.

"That's so generous of the team!" Uncle Zhang exclaimed. "Can we come over to watch the interview tomorrow?"

"Sure! It's at seven p.m.," Mom said. "After my Math Cup competition."

"Good luck! You're going to kill it!"

"Thanks," she said, reaching for her pronunciation cards again as she hung up the phone.

"Hey, I think you're good," I told her. She'd been studying those cards so intensely all week. I wished she'd relax and take a bath in the guest room. Maybe pour some of those expensive bubbles the customers were always leaving behind.

But Mom shook her head. "I have to pronounce every term perfectly or the other coaches won't take me seriously."

I wondered if she was still thinking about the first day she substituted for our math class, and how Bethany Brett had laughed when Mom mispronounced *Pythagorean theorem*. I hoped the memory hadn't been bothering Mom all this time. But I also knew from reading Michael Yao's letters that we don't always get to choose when memories stop haunting us.

Slowly, I picked up one of her cards. If this was important to her, she didn't have to do it alone.

"Let's practice together. What do you call the distance across a circle?" I asked.

Mom looked up in surprise. "Diameter?"

I gave her a thumbs-up and flipped to the next card. "An equation with two terms?"

She thought for a second. "A binomial," she replied perfectly.

I nodded. We flew through the next thirty-five terms, and then I put the last card down and quizzed Mom on one more thing.

"What do you call a woman who came over from China many years ago, wasn't sure whether she could be a teacher in this country, but through her tireless effort is taking her team to the Math Cup? A woman who *deserves* a kitchen island, darn it?"

Mom smiled and put a hand over her heart. "Oh, Mia."

"You got this, Mom," I said, handing her back all her cards.

Mom and I hugged tightly. Then she headed out the back for her guest room, and I crawled into bed.

I hoped that tomorrow Lupe and Mom would snatch the trophy from Team Sentilla, and that the soccer team's interview would be a roaring success on TV. Most of all, I hoped Mom could see when she got there, it didn't matter how she pronounced the words. It was her passion and devotion to her students that made her a winner.

CHAPTER 56

At the Math Cup the next day, I was completely on edge, holding the corners of my Polaroid camera so hard I was afraid the plastic might crack. Mom kept an eagle eye on Team Sentilla. When one of them leaned over to get something from a backpack, Mom checked to make sure it was a water bottle, and not a calculator.

"Is this really necessary?" their coach snapped.

"You tell me," Mom replied.

He shook his head. "Demanding a rematch all because of a photograph? They weren't even *using* the calculator!"

"Oh, yeah, it happened to be lying just under the table, getting a tan," Mom said sarcastically. "Give me a break."

"Fine. We'll play along. You'll see, my kids will win again."

Mom ignored him.

"My kids are already graphing two-variable linear inequality," he continued. "Your kids know how to do that?"

Mom's nostrils flared as she shot back, "Of course they do. They can convert between exponential and logarithmic form, find the inverse of a matrix, the vertex of a parabola, *and* calculate the inverse of a cosin."

Oh, no. Mom was so fired up, she'd accidentally mispronounced cosin as "cousin."

The Sentilla Beach coach roared with laughter. "Cousin??" he asked. "I *hope* they can find their cousin!"

Mom turned beet red.

"And you call yourself a math coach!"

The judges cleared their throats, prompting us to quiet down and look over—to see Lupe with her hand raised. The air stilled. I felt my heart leap practically out of my body as I jumped up in the air—they were done! *YES!!!!*

The Sentilla Beach coach went pale. We all held our breaths as the judges checked our team's work. Finally, the senior judge tapped on the mic.

"Looks like we have a winner!" he declared.

Mom and I ran over to the team, and I hugged my best friend. We squished the Polaroid camera hanging from my neck, but I didn't care.

"Congratulations, Team Anaheim! You're the new champions of the Math Cup, Orange County!" he declared.

Team Sentilla threw all their pencils on the floor, they were so mad. But it didn't matter. We won!

Lupe turned to her team as I snapped pictures. "We did it!!!" she yelled.

"You were an incredible team captain," Allie said. Ethan, Noah, and Ben all took turns high-fiving Lupe.

"It was *all* of us," Lupe corrected. "Teamwork makes the dream work!"

Mom gave each of them a big hug. "I'm so, so proud of you!" she said. Then she pulled six World Cup tickets from her purse and handed them out.

I took a picture of Team Sentilla's faces. Their mouths hung open like one long parenthesis.

"Is that . . . ?" they asked.

"A World Cup ticket!" Lupe beamed. "How's that for a trophy?"

Ethan, Ben, and the rest of the team laughed as they walked over to pick up their actual Cup trophy. I held my camera high as Mom put her arms around her students. With a mischievous smile, I instructed the team to smile on the count of three.

"One, two, three, *cousin*!" I shouted proudly.

. . .

That night, we all gathered around the TV in the manager's quarters to watch my big interview with the Chinese women's soccer team. I was sandwiched between Uncle Zhang and Aunt Ling, while Mom sat next to Dad in the living room, and Lupe sat next to her mom. Mrs. Garcia had brought over a big bowl of homemade guacamole, and we were dipping tortilla chips in it. Jason walked in with another appetizer, something new that Hank had been working on.

I reached for one of the crispy wrapped mini hot dogs.

"I'm calling them pigs in a towel," Hank said with a grin. He told me how he'd wrapped them in pretzel dough. I was so proud of him for continuing to innovate and putting the whole Pasadena Grill ordeal behind him. I knew it wasn't easy.

"You're an amazing chef, you know that? You warm us all up with your food."

Hank put his hand over mine. "Thanks," he said. "That's all I've ever wanted. And I don't need my name on a fancy menu to prove it. I've been doing that all along right here."

"You certainly have, partner," Jason said, passing around the delicious pigs in a towel.

I was glad to have both our talented chefs back under one roof. As we settled down on the sofa, the *CBS News* theme song started playing.

"Here it is!!" Mom shouted.

Liane's smiling face flashed onto the screen. There was a whoop of joy when the team and I came on.

"Tonight, we sit down exclusively with the Chinese women's soccer team. Here to translate for them is local student journalist Mia Tang," Liane started.

Jason threw his arms up, accidentally knocking over Hank's platter and sending all the pigs in a towel flying. I laughed.

"Leave 'em!" Hank said. "Let's watch!"

We all leaned close to the screen. I thought I'd sound like a squeaky mouse on TV, but to my surprise, I spoke clearly and confidently.

Dad threw his arms around me when it was over. "You were amazing!"

"You really did such a good job, Mia," Mrs. Garcia agreed. "You were so calm and poised. So comfortable, and proud. Brava!"

Lupe turned to her mom. "Hey, there's something I have to talk to you about. . . ."

As Lupe and her mom went to find a quiet place, I heard the front desk phone ringing. I ran over to answer.

"Mia!" my cousin's voice greeted me.

"Shen!" I cried. Finally, he was back! There was so much I had to tell him! "How was Sanya?"

"Amazing!" he said. "But not as amazing as what you've been up to! I saw your column in the middle school *Gazette*!"

I beamed. "It was incredible, Shen! I even interviewed them on TV! I'll send you a tape!"

"Wow! Yeah, send it so I can show my classmates! They keep saying you were making it up; there's no way a kid could get an interview with a major soccer team," Shen said. "I told them you don't know my cuz!"

I laughed.

It had been a pretty incredible couple of weeks. I was so glad I hadn't given up. Through my digging, I discovered so much, not just about the amazing World Cup players, but also about Mr. Yao's past. Most of all, I'd discovered that both of my halves could flourish in me. That both sides of me were valid.

"Mia! Time for dinner!" Mom called.

I promised to give Shen a minute-by-minute recap after the big game. "Oh, and one more thing—what's the number of that *dofunao* place?" I asked. "By Lao Lao's house?"

"I don't know," Shen said, "but I'll find out!"

Hanging up the phone, I skipped over to the kitchen to join my family and friends. Lupe and her mom were sitting next to each other at the dining table. Mrs. Garcia was giving my best friend a massive hug. I sighed with relief—obviously their talk had gone well.

Then Jason and Hank walked out with a feast. There was spaghetti Bolognese, cheesy shrimp spring rolls, roasted pumpkin frittata, and roasted pork belly with hoisin sauce.

"Eat up!" Mom said. "Tomorrow, we're making history!"

CHAPTER 57

Lupe came over bright and early the next morning so we could get ready for the big match together. Mr. Antwell had called me even earlier in the morning to wish the team good luck. He also said he'd seen the interview and was proud of me.

"You got here because you kept your eye on the ball and you didn't give up until you landed on prime time," he said.

"Thanks for helping me realize what sports are really about," I told him.

Lupe and I put on matching red shirts, just like Gao Hong and Sun Wen were wearing. Then with a white correction marker we drew stripes like the Adidas logo.

Lupe modeled her finished shirt in the mirror.

"So what'd your mom say?" I asked.

"She said whatever I decided, we'd figure it out. And that she and my dad love me, always."

I took her hand and looked into her eyes. "All of us love you always."

Lupe smiled. "You think Allie's going to like this? Or will she think it's weird?" she asked, pointing to her decorated shirt.

"Course she's going to like it! Why pay for stripes when you have a Wite-Out marker?"

Lupe giggled.

We then headed over to my dresser, where we searched for white scrunchies. We were wearing white socks, white shorts, and white scrunchies for Team USA. I looked in the mirror and smiled at the two halves of me, perfectly represented.

Mom knocked on my door and called, "Hurry up! The traffic's going to be horrendous. We gotta go now!"

"Coming!" I grabbed my reporter's notebook and camera, and Lupe grabbed the water bottles—it was supposed to be 102 degrees that day!

Outside, Hank was checking the air on his tires, while Billy Bob was moving an ice cooler to his truck. He was wearing a red shirt too, with matching bright red athletic socks that went all the way to his thighs. I giggled.

There was a double honk as Uncle Zhang's and Aunt Ling's cars rolled in. Everybody was here, except Allie and Jason, who were meeting us at the stadium.

"You guys ready?" Dad asked.

Everyone nodded. Mom turned to Mrs. T, who'd agreed to stay behind to watch over the motel, and said, "Remember, if anyone wants a room, make sure you get their—"

"IDs and a key deposit, I got it. I've been practicing for when you guys stay at your house at night!" Mrs. T said with a smile.

Mom glanced at Dad.

"You guys still thinking about Maple Hills?" Hank asked.

My parents nodded.

"I know it's scary. But once you're in there, you're not even going to think about your neighbor," Hank said in his experienced-homeowner voice. "Can't let one narrow-minded guy stop you!"

Mom gave Hank a half smile as she got into her car.

"Maybe Hank's right," Dad said as she drove. "We should talk to an agent."

"We'd have to find another one willing to take us on," Mom said. "And that's not so easy."

I gazed out the window, mind spinning with things to do. Call real estate agents. Call up Maple Hills. But I told myself I could do all that tomorrow.

Today, I would cheer my heart out and celebrate the historic accomplishment that my two halves were playing each other at the World Cup. The closer we got to the Rose Bowl, the harder my chest thumped, until I could hardly stand it anymore.

Turning into the Rose Bowl parking lot, I pressed my nose up against the back window. Row after row of cars waited to get into the lot, as ninety thousand fans made their way to the stadium. I snapped a picture. Never in my entire life had I seen so many people all in one place before.

"Holy moly!" Lupe cried, jumping out of the car. I spotted Jason getting dropped off by Mr. Yao and waved. Lupe's parents ran over toward us and joined their daughter. We all followed the crowd, with Mom and Dad close behind us.

"This is incredible!" Jason said. "I've never seen so many people at a game before, not even at a Lakers game on TV!"

When we got up to the gate, I saw most of the fans were wearing white USA shirts. There were several guys carrying *I Love You, Mia Hamm* posters. They had lipstick marks on their foreheads. Allie and Lupe rolled their eyes. I looked around and saw American flags draping from several necks. The sight of the American flag always made my heart swell, and today was no exception.

We spotted Hank and waved at the rest of the weeklies and Uncle Zhang and Auntie Ling. As we waited for them to come over, a large congregation of people started chanting, "USA! USA!" I took another picture.

Hank came over, and we flashed our tickets. Walking inside, we were shocked to find our seats were *super* close to the field.

"Best seats in the house!" Hank clapped his hands.

Then I noticed that a sizable number of people next to us were wearing red shirts too. Many of them were Asian American, but Team China had white, Black, and Latinx fans as well!

"They must have seen your interview!" Hank said.

"You think so?"

José, Lupe's dad, nodded. "They're rooting for the underdog!"

"That's the power of telling a story!" Hank smiled.

My mom gazed at the fans, equally stunned. As the spectators around us waved the Chinese flag, I bumped her shoulder lightly with mine.

"See that, Mom? Not everyone wants to keep us out."

Mom got up and started waving too. She didn't have a flag, so she waved the next best thing she had in her purse—a postcard of the Calivista. And in a way, that was a sort of flag, because it was a celebration of all of us, from all different colors and backgrounds, living harmoniously together.

Then the teams made their way onto the field and the fans went *wild*. I got up and started screaming along with the crowd. As I rooted for the half of me that so rarely got any positive attention in this country, a swell of people behind me joined in. "Go, Team China!" we shouted.

I spotted Sun Wen running onto the field. I leaned forward and screamed the last line from her poem in Mandarin.

"'Come on, girls, do not wait to follow your dreams!'" I cheered.

I hoped Sun Wen's heart vibrated with the eager screams of so many girls who saw themselves out on the field for the first time ever. I hoped her legs felt the strength of their hope. Most of all, I hoped her fingers tingled with the possibility and promise of what this moment meant for womankind.

As the game kicked off, I could hear the adrenaline pounding in my ears.

CHAPTER 58

One hundred and twenty tense minutes later, the game was still a scoreless draw. Both teams had played so brilliantly that not a single ball had made it into either goal all afternoon.

For the last ten minutes, my throat was parched from screaming, and my mom chewed one of her nails to the quick. Then the World Cup officially went into penalty kicks. We all held our breaths.

"This is it. We're going into sudden death!" Hank hollered, gripping the bar next to our seats so tight, a coat of paint was coming off.

Next to us, I heard some other fans speculating.

"It's going to get hairy," one guy said.

"Who do you think's gonna run out of gas first?" another woman asked her husband. "The Chinese or the Americans?"

"Definitely the Chinese. I mean, just look at them—"

Jason and I both turned around in our seats, clearing our throats. "What *exactly* are you saying?" I asked.

The couple immediately quieted down. "Never mind," the husband said.

I turned my attention back to the game, sitting on the edge of my seat as Xie Huilin walked toward the ball. "C'mon," I screamed, pumping my fist in the air.

Mom was so nervous, she closed her eyes. "You watch for me," she whispered.

So I watched with my eyes doubly open as Xie Huilin shot the ball straight into the goal! Score!

Thunderous cheering erupted from our section of the stadium. Jason, Lupe, and I high-fived as Mom opened her eyes.

Someone called out, "Do the wave! Do the wave!" I looked back and saw people standing up and down next to one another, and I immediately grabbed my parents. Lupe grabbed her parents. And we did our first ever American wave!

Up next was Carla Overbeck, who shot one in for the US. The crowd went wild, and Jason gobbled up a whole bag of popcorn, he was so excited. Two more penalty shots later, the stadium erupted again when goalie Briana Scurry saved a shot from Liu Ying.

Mom and I turned to each other and gulped.

"That's one down for China," Mom said.

"Have hope, have hope!" Hank urged.

It had all come down to Brandi Chastain. If she kicked the ball in, Team USA would clinch victory! As Brandi Chastain ran up to the goal, the entire stadium went quiet. As she kicked the ball, Gao Hong threw herself onto the grass to save it, but the ball sailed past her.

Team USA won!

Brandi Chastain screamed and took off her jersey. As her teammates ran toward her, the stadium exploded.

A heavy, bittersweet feeling sank into my stomach as Mom pulled me in for a hug.

"Next time!" she said.

I nodded and wiped the tears from my eyes. Lupe pointed at the Chinese players. They were gazing up at the stadium. They seemed like they were just taking it in. Like after all that playing, they finally had a moment to look up.

Lupe, Jason, and I started running toward the field. Team USA was swamped with fans, but there was nobody around Team China. We hopped over the divider and ran up to our heroes.

"You guys were amazing!" I cried.

"Not amazing enough to stop the ball," Gao Hong sighed. Sun Wen patted her shoulder, but I could tell Gao Hong was taking it hard.

Liu Ying, who missed the penalty kick, pointed up to the stadium. "It's all the noise. So many fans. I got distracted."

I could tell they were crushed by their defeat. It was *so* close. It must have been hard playing with so much thunderous clapping. But the fact that ninety thousand people showed up . . . that must have felt good.

"Ninety thousand!" I told Liu Yang. "Never before in sports history have that many people turned up for a women's event. *That's* a victory in and of itself!"

Gao Hong smiled. "It sure is," she said.

The players waved to all their fans in the upper rows wearing red jerseys and shouting their names. Folks from all walks of life and ethnicities had turned up for these women because they saw themselves in their struggle.

"Thank you!" Gao Hong shouted in English.

"We love you!" a woman shouted back in Spanish.

"We love you too!" Sun Wen called back.

Lupe looked over at her parents, who had come down to the field with my mom and dad. They gave her a warm snuggle. *We love you*, they mouthed to her. I smiled.

"Hey, you guys hungry?" Jason asked Gao Hong.

Gao Hong put her goalie glove over her stomach. "Are you kidding? I could eat five hundred dumplings."

Jason grinned. "Good, because I know just the place around here!"

As we started walking over to the team bus together, I gazed at the packed stadium one last time. Ninety thousand screaming fans—I hoped the Chinese team's ears rang for a long, long time. They scored their goal of elevating women's soccer and then some!

CHAPTER 59

That night, we packed into Lotus Garden, where we ordered thirteen different types of dumplings. Mr. Yao drove over with his wife and so did Lupe's parents and Allie's, and we managed to polish off every last bamboo basket.

"This place sure brings back memories," Mr. Yao said. He pointed to the small goldfish on his teacup and told Jason he still remembered buying the cups with his dad. "I wanted to get these modern gray ones, but your grandfather insisted on these. They were on sale. Ninety-nine cents for two."

Jason smiled at the goldfish. "I like these too," he said. "They're more traditional."

Mr. Yao put the teacup down. "When I was your age, I wanted to get far away from traditional—from anything remotely Chinese. But you, you lean into it." He paused. "And that makes me proud."

Jason lifted his teacup and clinked his dad's. I held up my own goldfish and turned to the players, standing up.

"I want to say a toast. Thank you for playing your hearts out today. For showing us we *can* and *deserve* to be center stage."

Lupe stood up beside me and added, "For teaching us never to give up." She held up her own cup. "No matter how big our dreams are!"

"To be true to ourselves," Allie said, with a timid look over at her parents.

"And follow our passions!" Jason cheered, popping a dumpling into his mouth.

"Hear, hear!" Hank called.

Sun Wen put a hand over her heart as everyone in the room held up their teacups. We drank to their incredible achievement and the mark they'd left on soccer and on all of us forever.

. . .

Later, as I helped Mr. and Mrs. Wong pass out dessert, I saw my mom take out the Maple Hills flyer from her purse to show Gao Hong.

"This is the house we're thinking of buying," she told her in Chinese.

"Wow! That's a beautiful home!" Gao Hong said. She pointed at the lush green front lawn. "You could put a nice soccer pitch right there!"

Mom laughed, exchanging a look with Dad.

"Bet our new neighbor will love that," he joked.

"But you know what I realized today?" Mom said. "There might be some who want to keep us out, but there are far more people who want us to play."

I bounced on the balls of my feet. "Does that mean we're buying the place??" I asked, so excited I almost dropped the almond cookies.

"We have to find a real estate agent first," Mom answered.

Mr. Yao pointed to the flyer. "You guys need a real estate agent? I know a good one! I can introduce you. He'll help you land the house."

"Really?" Mom asked Mr. Yao. She looked amazed as Mr. Yao jotted down his realtor's number on the back of a napkin, and I thought I caught a glimpse of young Michael Yao. It made me poke Jason and smile.

Mrs. Wong tapped on my shoulder. "By the way," she said, "I found another old letter after you left. Back in the kitchen."

I wiped the almond cookie crumble off my hands and followed. She pulled out a small package from the kitchen drawer by the chef's station. It was bulkier than the other letters.

Carefully, I opened it.

Inside, I found two tickets. They were plane tickets from Los Angeles to London for Lishing Yao and Bu Fu Yao. Michael's parents were planning on coming to see him!

I looked behind the tickets. There was a cassette tape. I took it out. On the back of the tape was a handwritten label:

TRUMPET MUSIC FROM THE RADIO. FOR MICHAEL.

"Mr. Yao!" I yelled, running out to the dining room with the tape and the tickets.

The room stilled as Mr. Yao opened the letter. I wished I could describe the emotions on his face as he registered the contents. Knowing his parents had planned to come to London. They'd bought the tickets. They'd been listening to the radio, recording the parts with a trumpet playing. They were proud of him.

On that fateful day, the pain and regret of his past finally lifted. And what flooded in was love.

CHAPTER 60

Three weeks later, I was polishing off a new piece entitled "Rooting for My Roots" for the school newspaper when the phone rang. I almost didn't hear it at first, over Mr. Yao's beautiful trumpet playing next door at the restaurant. You'd never believe that man could make such beautiful music, but his old band teacher was right. His playing reminded me of Louis Armstrong, and we were lucky to have him.

"Calivista Motel. How can I help you?" I answered.

"Is this Mia Tang?" a woman asked.

"Yup!" I answered.

"I'm calling from the *San Francisco Tribune*."

I sucked in a breath.

"My name is Kimmy Flores, and I'm the editor in charge of our winter journalism camp. We were very impressed with your coverage of the FIFA Women's World Cup, and we'd like to extend a full scholarship to you to attend our journalism program this winter."

I screamed so loudly, Mr. Yao came running over with his trumpet.

"What's going on?" he asked.

"I got in!!!" I told him.

As I thanked Ms. Flores and got off the phone with her, Mr. Yao held up his trumpet and started playing "La Vie en Rose."

"That's what I played when I found out I was going to Europe," he said between breaths.

I swayed gently to the music, feeling nostalgic already. As excited as I was to go to San Francisco, I also knew I was going to miss everyone so much. Especially this year, when we could finally celebrate Christmas together in front of the fireplace at our new house. Two days before, our offer for the town house in Maple Hills had been accepted. We were really buying our first American house!

At the thought of spending my first Christmas away from my pup, Comma, I got really quiet.

"Was it hard going so far away?" I asked Mr. Yao.

He stopped playing and shook his head. "No, because you're already there." He pointed to his head. "You've been living there a long time."

I smiled. It was so true. In my mind, I'd already gotten into the journalism camp a hundred times. I'd biked up and down the Golden Gate Bridge and ridden on the cable cars. I was already *there*.

"You owe it to your dreams to go there in real life. *And*," Mr. Yao added, "no matter where you go, home will always be right here." He patted his chest.

"Thanks, Mr. Yao."

Who knew such wise words could come from such an ex-grump! Then again, I had a stack of letters in my room to prove he knew what he was talking about. As he headed back to the diner, I went to tell my parents and Hank the good news.

Dad was in Mom's guest room, packing up all her stuff for the big move.

"Dad! Guess what?" I exclaimed.

"You decided you want a little terrier and not a beagle?" he asked.

"Oh, no, I still want a beagle! But I might have to wait until after Christmas. I got into the *San Francisco Tribune* camp!"

Dad dropped the packing tape. "That's my girl!" he exclaimed. "I'm so proud of you!"

Hank ran in with a copy of the *Anaheim Times* in his hands.

"Have you guys seen this?!"

He pointed at the headline in the Food section: "Fresh from Their World Cup Win, Team USA Declares the Best Burger in Los Angeles—at Anaheim's Calivista Motel!"

Hank stared at us. "How did this happen? I don't remember them ever coming into the restaurant!"

I grinned. "Remember when you said we should send Jason's duck to the Anaheim Ducks?" I asked.

Hank put two and two together. "You sent my burger to *Mia Hamm*?" he shrieked, picking me up for a bear hug.

"I might have!" I said, squealing. "I couldn't be objective, but I figured *everyone* would listen to Team USA's review!"

He spun me around and around. Then I dug into my pocket for another surprise. "Oh, and here! Before I forget!"

Hank's eyes boggled at the seven cool Benjamins I handed him.

"I called the *dofunao* restaurant owner. That's your cut, from using your recipe. And they'll be sending you more every month."

"You're kidding! Now I can pay back the loan on my condo!" Hank slapped his knee.

Dad cut in. "She hasn't even told you the biggest news of all! Mia got into journalism camp!"

"You're going to San Francisco???" Hank asked.

As I nodded, Hank threw his cash up in the air. A confetti of dreams and excitement fell around us as we laughed and celebrated.

We were still laughing when Mom's car pulled into the lot. We all ran out. Mom and Lupe had been at the regional Math Cup competition in Los Angeles all day—we were dying to know the result.

"Guess what?" Lupe shrieked, getting out of the car. "We won! We're heading to the state champions for the Math Cup in December!"

"And guess where it's gonna be?" Mom added. "In San Francisco!"

I screamed again. "That's where my journalism camp is! I got in!"

Lupe and I started jumping up and down in the lot. Ready or not, San Francisco, here we come!

A plane flew overhead as we jumped, and Lupe and I looked up. I wondered if the soccer players were on it. I thought of the last line from Sun Wen's poem. *Come on, girls, do not wait to follow your dreams.*

Smiling, I whispered to the plane, "We won't! We're going for them full speed!" And though there may be bumps in the road, and some days it might feel like the goal is a million miles away, we're not stopping until we get there!

AUTHOR'S NOTE

Meeting the Chinese women's national football team was as much a thrill for me as it was for Mia!

When I was fourteen years old and a young, eager student reporter, I read about a soccer match that was happening in my town. Not just any soccer match—the FIFA Women's World Cup! The year was 1999. Team China was playing Team USA!

Now, I was not a soccer fanatic in the traditional sense (like Mia, I struggled in PE most of my life and had a profound fear of balls). But the idea of seeing female athletes who looked like me playing in the FIFA World Cup Finals fired me up. Rumor had it that the goalie on the Chinese team worked in a factory as a kid. I thought she'd get a kick out of the fact that I worked in a motel, so I was determined to get an interview. The only problem was that no one knew where Team China was staying.

They were hunkered down in their hotel in Pasadena somewhere and were saying no to all interview requests. But like Mia, I believed where there's a will, there's a way! So for the next few weeks, I made my parents drive me to every hotel and restaurant in Pasadena. My parents would wait outside in the car, and I would run inside the lobby and look for Chinese people. I was determined to find the team!

Soccer fever was spreading throughout the Los Angeles area, with posters and billboards of Mia Hamm and Brandi Chastain springing up all over the city. Around school, more and more kids were wearing soccer jerseys supporting Team USA.

But I was laser-focused on getting my interview with Team China. Finally, after weeks of searching, I spotted a Chinese man in an Adidas tracksuit sitting in the lobby of a hotel reading a newspaper. It turned out he was the coach of the team! I'll never forget the feeling of seeing the elevator doors open and my favorite soccer stars walk out. I ran up to them and asked if I could have an interview. They were so gracious and kind, spending hours talking to me. Hearing their stories, I was so blown away by the courage and resilience it took for these women to get to the World Cup. Many of the conversations in this book with Gao Hong and Sun Wen were real.

What was also real, though, was the rising anti-Chinese sentiment in the weeks leading up to the big match. Local paper headlines started getting noticeably more hostile (not to mention sexist). Like Mia, I was called a "traitor" by my school counselor when I excitedly told him about my interview. I was heartbroken. I'd worked so hard to prove myself, and to be accepted in this country. Yet, with one comment, it felt like everything I'd accomplished could get wiped out. As I counted down to the big day, I wondered if the stadium—and the United States—had room for both the Chinese and the American parts of me.

My greatest hope in writing *Key Player* is for kids to understand there *is* room. There's room for all the parts of you. All your history and hopes and dreams, and things you're still figuring out too. The 1999 World Cup taught me that.

Here were some of my columns about this pivotal game:

Women's World Cup '99: The Chinese Perspective
By Kelly Yang

Editor's Note—Staff Writer Kelly Yang obtained an exclusive opportunity to interview the Chinese Women's National Football (Soccer) Team before and after the Finals of the 1999 FIFA Women's World Cup. The quotes from the team members in this article were translated from Chinese by Yang.

For the Chinese team and their fans, it was more than a simple game of soccer at the Rose Bowl in Pasadena Saturday, July 10, as the final match of the FIFA Women's World Cup pitted China against the US and the loss was felt on many levels.

There was a lot at stake. Officials said that the financial situation of the Chinese team was shaky. The team was partly sponsored by Adidas, but outside of their expenses, the pay for some players bordered on nothing. Winning the World Cup meant not only gaining the title of being "the best" but also an extra $10,000 for each player.

But whether the team wins or not, the already remarkable success of the women's soccer team marks a great achievement for Chinese women and the image of all of womankind.

Gao Hong, the "golden goalkeeper," Forward and Team Captain Sun Wen, and their teammates said that they were particularly happy to be here in America playing in the final match, which they came such a long way for.

Me with Gao Hong in 1999

"We are excited about the game. We want to win for China and for womankind," Gao said in Chinese.

The success of the women's soccer team marks a great achievement for Chinese women. She knows this more than anyone. At the young age of ten, she began a career in soccer, often practicing with boys while perfecting techniques on her own. Sun said one of the key people who inspired her success was her father. Her father and coach helped her out in difficult times, when she wanted to quit the sport.

"Most fathers in China cannot accept girls playing soccer," Sun said. "It's the culture. Girls are supposed to be shy and steady and not so active."

As Sun points out, women's sports have only recently been publicly approved in the Chinese culture. This year's World Cup championship is especially important because it proves to a country that once did not think that women were good enough to play soccer that women can and are able to achieve equally to men. It is a milestone in Chinese women's history.

Despite tremendous pressure on the team, the Chinese team was not nervous the day before the game. Sun, along with a handful of other players, were jumping around with great confidence.

"The ball's going in tomorrow," Sun shouted excitedly. "We're going to try as hard as we possibly can. We're going to give it all we got!"

The Chinese Women's Soccer Team: The Impossible Interview
By Kelly Yang

"I win," I screamed as I exited the hotel where the Chinese Women's Soccer Team was staying. I had just finished interviewing the soccer player Gao Hong and her other teammates! As I sat in the car still processing the incredible interview, I felt like the happiest little girl in the entire world! I had accomplished the impossible—I had interviewed one of my greatest heroes!

The whole meeting was a miracle! I had spent weeks trying to find the team, by going into various hotels. Finally, I figured out which hotel they were staying at by looking closely at the pictures of the players in various newspapers. I decided the best time to go would be before the players had dinner. They were bound to come down to the lobby to go to the restaurant!

Driving over to the hotel, I still had my doubts as to whether I could get the interview. I thought, "There's no way these players are going to talk to a young reporter like me." However, like everything else, I marched forward regardless of any hesitations I had.

When I arrived at the hotel, I immediately noticed an Asian man sitting next to a lady wearing a soccer uniform. I automatically thought that this pair must be associated with the team. As I explained to the man that I was a reporter and that I would like to interview the Chinese soccer players, he informed me that there were no reporters allowed! I was greatly disappointed. I felt like it was indeed hopeless that I would ever get to interview the Chinese soccer team.

As the man kept rejecting my every request, I grew more and more sad. To my surprise, the players started coming down for dinner. The elevator doors opened and to my delight, there they were! I immediately recognized Gao Hong, the goalie. I ran over and started talking to her. As she and her teammates talked, I asked her about her life and got a great interview! Miss Hong is a fascinating young woman who is one of the nicest people I'd ever met. She made me feel very comfortable and answered all my questions patiently. As I took pictures and got autographs from the players, I felt a great sense of pride. For me, this World Cup competition isn't just a celebration for Chinese athletes, it's also an honor for women!

I still have my copies of the LA Times *that covered the match!*

ACKNOWLEDGMENTS

My heartfelt thanks to the following people: my agent, Tina Dubois, who has been a tireless champion of Mia and the entire Calivista crew throughout all my books; my editor, Amanda Maciel, for your incredible editorial insight on every Front Desk book, but especially this one—I am so so proud of this book!—and to the greater Scholastic team, including Ellie Berger, Talia Seidenfeld, David Levithan, Alex Kelleher-Nagorski, Lauren Donovan, Taylan Salvati, Erin Berger, Rachel Feld, Lizette Serrano, Emily Heddleson, Lisa McClatchy, and Melissa Schirmer. Thank you for being such a loving home for this series!

I'm speechless with gratitude to Maike Plenzke and Maeve Norton for the incredible cover! It's been such a joy watching Mia grow up with you two!

To my greater ICM team, Alicia Gordon, Ava Greenfield, Tamara Kawar, Roxane Edouard, Isobel Gahan, Annabel White, and Savanna Wicks—thank you for bringing Mia to the world! Thanks to my publishers around the globe—Knights Of, Walker Books, Kim Dong, Dipper, Omnibook, Porteghaal, Albin Michel, Grupo SM, Wydawnictwo Poznańskie, and Kodansha!

Major thanks to my mom, who patiently drove me around that hot summer in 1999 so I could investigate every hotel in Pasadena, looking for the soccer teams. Thank you to my dad, who bought me every single newspaper—even though they cost three dollars each!—so I could read the headlines about the teams every day.

Much love to my own soccer fans, Tilden, Eliot, and Nina—thanks for cheering Mommy on. And to my husband, Stephen, an amazing athlete who, strangely enough, married someone completely uncoordinated.

Last but not least, thank you to all the librarians and teachers who have booktalked or taught the Front Desk series over the years. You are the key players in my life! Thank you for believing in me, for cheering me on, for having my back, even amid book bans and other challenges—it's been quite a roller coaster this last year! I wouldn't be here without you and it is the greatest honor of my life to be able to write for you.